ON THIN ICE...

I noticed a light-haired guy as he skated onto the ice. He looked more confident than any other guy skater I knew. He was wearing old gray sweatpants with a stretched-out black turtleneck that made his light eyes glow. This guy was big for a skater. In fact, he looked as if he belonged on the football team with my boyfriend, Troy. And he was definitely as hot as Troy—hotter maybe.

He skated smoothly around the ice, gathering speed with each step he took. I couldn't take my eyes off him. Then, suddenly, he took off into an impossibly high jump. It was only a single axel, one and a half rotations in the air from a forward takeoff. And he didn't hold his arms quite right. But he was so high that he seemed to hang there, suspended in midair. It was as if gravity had no effect on him. Sometimes I jumped like that in my dreams, but never in real life.

"Who's that?" I blurted out before I could stop myself.

"That's Kai Bergstrom."

Don't miss any of the books in *Love Stories*
—the romantic series from Bantam Books!

Who Do You LOVE?

Janet Quin-Harkin

BANTAM BOOKS
NEW YORK · TORONTO · LONDON · SYDNEY · AUCKLAND

RL 6, age 12 and up

WHO DO YOU LOVE?
A Bantam Book / October 1996

Produced by Daniel Weiss Associates, Inc.
33 West 17th Street
New York, NY 10011.

ISBN: 0-553-57043-9

Published simultaneously in the United States and Canada

Bantam Books are published by Bantam Books, a division of Bantam
Doubleday Dell Publishing Group, Inc. Its trademark, consisting of the
words "Bantam Books" and the portrayal of a rooster, is Registered in
U.S. Patent and Trademark Office and in other countries. Marca
Registrada. Bantam Books, 1540 Broadway, New York, New York 10036.

PRINTED IN THE UNITED STATES OF AMERICA

OPM   0 9 8 7 6 5 4

ONE

I'LL NEVER FORGET the day I met Troy Woodson—captain of the football team and the coolest guy at Berkeley High.

I guess I'm still a little in shock that a gorgeous, popular guy like Troy chose me as his girlfriend. It's not that I'm a loser or anything. In fact, I think I'm kind of cute when I take time with my appearance, which I rarely do. I'm petite—barely five three. And I look younger than sixteen, especially when I wear my long brown hair up in a ponytail. I used to love when my hair streaked blond in the summer, but that was before I spent every waking moment at the skating rink.

My dream is to become an Olympic figure skater. And my coach, Myra Richards, says it's good to look young. Sometimes the judges are easier on younger skaters and overlook their mistakes.

Anyway . . . I'm definitely not what you'd call

popular—and there are plenty of popular girls at Berkeley High School. Actually I'm kind of shy when I'm off the ice. And my crazy life is so filled with skating that I don't have time to do normal high-school things—like going to football games, hanging out with friends, or meeting guys.

My skating was what brought me and Troy together. Most people who knew about my life thought I was insane to get up before five every morning and spend so much time at the rink.

"You really think you've got a chance to make the Olympics?" they'd ask, seeming as if they were trying hard not to grin.

And I always answered, "Absolutely!" with the most confident smile I could produce.

It was thanks to that confidence that our local paper decided to feature me in a special story. One day about a month ago they sent a reporter and photographer to my school, as well as to the ice rink. "A DAY IN THE LIFE OF A RISING STAR," they'd called it.

It was hard not to notice me that day, with a reporter and photographer following me everywhere. And since I'm so small, the reporter guy thought it might be fun to photograph me next to a stud from the football team.

"So who's the star football player?" the reporter had asked me as we'd walked across to the football field. I'd told him about Troy—that he was the star quarterback and captain of the team—and he decided to caption the photo TWO

NAMES TO WATCH OUT FOR. KIRSTEN AND TROY—SPORTS STARS OF THE FUTURE.

I'd snuck a glance at Troy's dark good looks. His hair had fallen into his eyes, and he'd blushed bright red. I remember thinking it had made him seem human and not just an idol to drool over.

"Stars of the future, huh?" Troy had nudged me as if we were sharing a secret joke.

"Sure. Why not?" I'd answered. Then I'd added boldly, "I'll come to your Super Bowl if you come to my Olympics."

He'd held out his hand. "You've got a deal."

After the shooting had ended, Troy had offered to drive me home. Of course I'd been smart enough to lie. . . . I wasn't about to tell him that my car was sitting in the school parking lot. I don't think I stopped grinning the entire ride home in Troy's black BMW.

"Do you ever have time for anything besides skating?" Troy had asked as he'd pulled up in front of my house a few minutes later. "Do you really skate every day?"

I remember nodding, my tongue tied at the excitement of being so close to Troy.

"That's cool," Troy had said. "I'm the same way about football." Then he'd invited me to a party.

That party had been the most special night of my life, even better than when I'd won my first real competition and I'd fallen asleep with my trophy wrapped in my arms. Troy had stuck to me like glue all evening, making me feel so special.

I practically floated home that night. And when Troy leaned close to me, pressing his warm lips against mine . . . well, I'd been afraid I'd explode! It was a magical kiss. Not that I'd had much experience in the kissing department. Troy had taken me tenderly into his arms, bringing his lips closer and closer to mine until they finally, gently touched. I'd thought I'd melt with happiness. Troy's lips were so warm, and his arms around me made me feel cherished and loved. I bet I could have done *quadruple* jumps that night.

Troy and I have been together ever since. And it's been totally amazingly great. For the first time I could remember, I had a life outside of skating. And I couldn't believe all that I had been missing.

Troy came into my life like a warm springtime breeze. He opened the world to me. I was no longer the lonely figure skater; suddenly I was a somebody at school. Kirsten Hayes—girlfriend of the most popular guy in school. Now when I walked through the halls with Troy's letter jacket draped around my shoulders, people stopped to say hello. Sometimes I still pinched myself when I sat beside Troy on the warm stone steps in front of the school or when he'd give me a special smile from the football field. If this was a dream, I didn't want it to end.

"Let's take it from the top," Myra said as I paused for breath.

"Excuse me?" I didn't think I'd heard her correctly. Surely she couldn't want me to go through the whole thing again. I'd already been skating for over two hours and my legs felt like jelly.

"From the top," she said calmly. "The whole routine, Kirsten, and this time let's see if we can do it without falling over."

"But Myra . . . ," I began. My afternoon practice at the rink was supposed to go from three-thirty to five-thirty. I snuck a glance at the clock above the hockey commentator's box. It was already after five-thirty, and I was pooped.

"Do you want to get that triple toe loop or don't you?" she asked.

"Sure I do, but . . . ," I stopped, frustrated.

Myra glided across the ice as easily as if she were walking across the street. I knew she'd ignored my complaints as I watched her rewinding the tape of music I had been skating to. I watched her fake-fur-coated back with something close to hate.

Myra was a sweet, grandmotherly lady. She never yelled. She was always calm, and she'd been my coach for as long as I could remember. But sometimes she bugged the heck out of me!

My mouth was as dry as sandpaper. And my legs didn't feel as if they could support me anymore. But I didn't say another word. If there's one thing I'd learned in eight years of skating, it was that there was no use arguing with Myra. She always got the last word. Besides, she was right. I did want to get that triple jump.

Myra had only started teaching me the triple toe loop a few weeks ago—around the time I met Troy—and it was still very difficult and exciting. I hadn't quite gotten the hang of it yet, but I was almost there—just another half turn in the air and I'd have it nailed!

And when I nailed it, I'd be one of the hot shots. I'd have a real chance at the Olympics. Triples weren't *required* elements in a routine, but they definitely caught a judge's eye. Land three triples in your routine and you had it made.

I'd learned that rule the hard way at Senior Nationals last spring. The year before I had won a bronze at Junior Nationals. So of course I had stars in my eyes as I boarded the plane to Providence with my mother and Myra to compete in Senior Nationals a few months ago. I had promised myself I wouldn't be disappointed if I didn't get a medal. Top six would have been fine. Then the year after I'd be a real contender, in time for the Olympics in '98.

But I had only come in eleventh. What a shock to my ego! I had gotten used to being a star. Being number one. I was the only skater at my level at my rink, and I had a shelf full of trophies I had won at local competitions, then Regionals and Junior Nationals.

After Providence, I knew I still had a long way to go. All the best skaters had triple jumps in their routines. It didn't matter that my line was perfect in my spiral or that my footwork in my dance-step sequence was the best. Triples were what mattered.

The fancy skating in between was just padding. One girl even fell on her rear and still placed higher than me because she landed an amazing triple.

And I had been learning it ever since. I couldn't believe how long it was taking me. Skating usually came so easily. At first it just annoyed me that I couldn't nail the triple toe loop. Now I was beginning to panic. I imagined triple jumps in my head during math class. I dreamed triple jumps in my sleep at night. Even while I was cuddling Troy! I knew I had to nail that triple soon or I could kiss the next Olympics good-bye.

I'd dreamed of the Olympics since I'd watched Katarina Witt win her second gold medal in 1988. She'd seemed like a fairy princess to me, the way she'd floated across the ice and twirled in the air as if she could fly. For weeks I'd bugged my mother to take me to an ice rink. Finally she gave in and I joined the Berkeley Blades—the local skating club where I live in Berkeley, California, across the bay from San Francisco.

The first moment I stepped out onto the ice, I knew I belonged there. Other kids teetered around, ankles wobbling and hands clutching at the barrier. But I sailed easily across that ice before the end of my first session.

Myra had approached my mother a few months after I'd begun skating, asking if she could coach me. She thought I had a natural talent, and she thought I had what it took to win the gold. Working with a coach was very different from Saturday mornings at the skating club. It meant going to the rink every morning before school for two hours on the ice. Then another two to three hours after school for ballet lessons and strength training in the gym. And it was going to cost my parents a lot of money.

My parents had sacrificed a lot for my skating. We're not rich, but my parents promised to work it out somehow if I really wanted to skate. I was prepared to work hard. More than anything I wanted to make my Olympic dreams come true. But I had no idea of the time and energy it would really take.

And now my goal was almost within my reach. Maybe by the next Olympics I'd be the next Kristi Yamaguchi, the next Michelle Kwan. Just as soon as I could do that triple. . . .

The opening bars of my music floated out across the ice. All the younger kids who took lessons moved to the side, and spectators peeked out of the snack bar to see what was going on. But I hardly noticed them. I was used to people watching me. I was the only top-level skater at the rink. Apart from me it was all younger kids, beginners.

I adjusted the gloves on my icy hands and closed my eyes, my mind totally focused on my routine. I was Kirsten Hayes, future Olympic star. Gracefully skating across the ice, my legs forgot how tired they were. I glided through the first thirty seconds and went for a double flip. It required a backward takeoff from my toe pick and then two full revolutions high in the air.

Then I was supposed to land cleanly on one foot.

I skated faster and faster until everything became a blur. My body felt loose and weightless. I whirled around, digging my toe pick into the ice again. With all my strength I sprang high into the air, pulling my arms in tightly and beginning my rotations. One. Two. Before I knew what had happened, I touched ground again—on one foot!

Great! I was skating perfectly! Myra would definitely be delighted. I'd be out of there before six!

Wait a second . . . six o'clock? Alarm bells went off in my head. Something to do with six o'clock that was important? I heard Troy's voice saying, "I'll swing by and pick you up at six, then, okay?" I saw him run his hand through his messy dark hair.

I had gathered speed, preparing myself for the triple jump that was coming up. I tried to focus, but I couldn't get Troy's angry face out of my mind. I thought of him standing outside my front door at home, upset that I wasn't there.

I pushed into my takeoff, felt the rush of cold air in my face as the world spun around me, and . . . a split second later I landed hard on my bottom.

"Oh, no!" I muttered. I was smarting from the fall, but my pride was hurting more. Now I was all too aware of people watching me from the sidelines, the little kids giggling. I staggered to my feet, red faced. *That was a triple jump!* I wanted to yell to them. *I'd like to see you try one.*

But instead I pretended I hadn't even noticed

them. I brushed the ice off my black wool tights with my gloved hands.

"You didn't get enough height," Myra said. "You went into the takeoff all wrong." She spread her hands wide as if I were a hopeless case. "How do you think you can land when you lean back like that?"

"Maybe I'm not getting up enough speed?"

"The speed was fine," she said. "You need more power from that takeoff leg." She looked at me as if she were considering. "I don't think we should try it again tonight. You're tired. I've already kept you late. Go home. Take a bath. Sleep. We'll work on it again in the morning."

I whipped on my white rubber skate guards and ran to the locker room on the other side of the rink. I could be home in fifteen minutes if the traffic wasn't too bad. Maybe I wouldn't even be superlate for Troy. I'd only had a car for two months, since my sixteenth birthday, and I'd promised my mom that I would drive carefully. *So much for promises,* I thought as I drove home as fast as I dared.

My heart was hammering and I found it hard to breathe. How could I have forgotten about our date? I just hoped I hadn't completely blown it with Troy.

I quickly looked at the time flashing on the dashboard of my blue Toyota. 6:10. Not too bad. Anybody could be ten minutes late. I swung into my street, pulled up behind Troy's black BMW, and jumped out to find him sitting with the window open and the radio blaring.

"Hi," I yelled over the beat of a rap song. "Sorry I'm a little late. Coach wouldn't let me off the ice tonight."

"No problem," he said, smiling, his perfect white teeth gleaming at me. "I just got here myself. Coach kept me late too, talking strategy. Hop in."

"Let me run inside and change."

"You look great," he said, opening the passenger-side door.

Feeling very self-conscious, I climbed in beside him. "But I'm wearing sweats. . . ."

Troy leaned over and gave me a kiss. It wasn't the knock-your-socks-off kind of kiss—you know, the kind that makes your heart pound and your palms sweat. No, recently Troy's kisses were more like the friendly kind—the kind you gave to your sister. I guessed every kiss couldn't be as amazing as our first kiss.

"We're only going bowling." Troy lowered the blaring radio.

"Bowling? I love bowling!"

Troy burst out laughing.

"What's so funny?" I asked, glad that the setting sun had hidden my blush.

"You are." He reached across to stroke my cheek before he drove off. "It's like you're from another planet sometimes—in a nice way, of

11

course. You made it sound like I'd just invited you to Hawaii . . . not bowling."

I shrugged. "You know I don't get to do stuff like that very often. I'm either skating or at school or trying to catch up on homework."

"Myra works you too hard," he said. "Coaches are a pain, aren't they? They think they own you."

"You can say that again," I agreed.

"Myra's got to understand that you've got a life outside of skating now, Kirsten," Troy said quietly as he made a left turn.

"Myra has to work me hard. It's the only way I'll be ready for Senior Nationals in February," I explained. I was allowed to gripe about my coach, but that didn't mean that Troy could too.

"There's such a thing as working *too* hard. You can burn out, you know?"

"Not me. I've got my sights set on the Olympics."

"It's great to be ambitious, Kirsten," Troy said. "I know how you feel. I want to make it to the pros too. But I also plan on enjoying life. All you think about is skating."

"I think about you quite a bit."

He laughed. Then he was suddenly serious. "But what if it's all for nothing, Kirsten? There are hundreds of girls all across America who want to go to the Olympics. What if you give up your chance to be a regular teenager, a chance to have fun, and you don't make the cut?"

"That's not an option. I'm going to make it."
What was Troy's problem? Why was he being
such a jerk?

"I just hope you don't get hurt, that's all. I
hope you're not wasting your time. So, are you
ready for Saturday's game?" He quickly changed
the subject. Troy must have realized he was beginning to upset me.

"Saturday?" I said cautiously. "What time?"

"The game starts at eleven-thirty."

"Gee, I'm sorry, Troy," I said, "but you know
what my Saturdays are like. There's public skate
from ten to twelve and then again from two to
four. That means I can get on the ice between
twelve and two o'clock. I might be able to make
it for the end of the game. . . ."

"Couldn't you skip practice just this once?"

"Skip practice?" I laughed nervously. "I can't skip
practice, Troy. Even a fever won't stop me. Once I
collided with another skater and got stitches in my
leg, but I was back on the ice the next day. Besides,
you won't play any differently if I'm there or not."

"Sure I will. You're my good-luck charm,
Kirsten. I feel great when I see you on the sidelines, cheering for me. I feel like I can do anything when you're around."

"You know I'd be there if I could, Troy." I
stared out the windshield. "But there's no way.
You have to understand that. I bet your coach
wouldn't let you skip football practice to come
watch me skate."

13

"That's different," he said. We were at a red light. Troy looked over at me, then continued, "If I wasn't there, the whole team couldn't practice."

I snuck a glance at him to see if he was joking, but he wasn't. He actually expected me to skip a practice just to watch a silly football game. "Look," I began, flipping through the radio stations. Troy's rap music was beginning to irritate me now. "I'll ask Myra and see what I can do, okay?" But I knew she'd never let me go.

Troy just nodded. He was extraquiet the rest of the way to the bowling alley.

I just sat there, biting my lip, fighting the anger that was burning inside. Troy shouldn't have expected me to skip practice to watch his game. I doubted he'd do the same for me. Why couldn't he understand? Skating meant everything to me . . . maybe even more than Troy did.

TWO

As I HAD suspected, Myra wouldn't talk about me missing Saturday's practice. I couldn't even cut it short.

"I don't understand, Kirsten. Don't you want to land that triple?" she demanded. Myra was at the edge of the rink, watching as I stretched on Thursday afternoon.

"It's just that my boyfriend . . . ," I began.

She made a grunting noise in her throat. "Boyfriend," she spat. "You don't have time for boyfriends right now. You have to choose—skating or boyfriend."

"That's not fair," I said, bending over and touching my toes. "Of course I want to skate. It's all I've ever wanted to do. But I'm a teenager, Myra. I have a right to want a normal life." We were all alone that afternoon—no one else was in the arena.

15

"Not if you plan to make it to the Olympics, you don't," she said. "Maybe I was wrong about you, Kirsten. Maybe you don't want it bad enough."

That hurt. Of course I wanted to skate in the Olympics. I wanted it so bad, I could taste it. Why was she making such a big deal over one lousy practice? It's not as if I'd ever asked to skip one before.

I stood up and headed out to the ice to do my warm-ups . . . to put Myra's words out of my mind. I glided around the rink, taking long, fluid strides. As I leaned into my skating leg, slowly building speed, I got lost in my own doubts. I remembered what Troy had said about all those other girls across America, working toward the same goal. What if he was right and I'd given up my entire high-school social life for nothing?

I circled the rink several times, gaining more power with each trip around. Until Troy, I had been completely sure of myself . . . of my skating. I wanted a shot at the Olympics, and I was totally focused on achieving that goal. Before I met Troy, nothing outside of skating had seemed important. But now suddenly I wanted to be a normal teenager. I wanted to be with Troy.

I felt really confused and I missed an easy axel. Trying not to lose all concentration, I propelled myself high into the air on the outside edge of my left skate blade. Pulling my arms tightly into my chest for momentum, I barely made the one and a half turns clockwise and landed poorly on two wobbly legs . . . instead of landing cleanly on only one foot.

"I don't know what you thought that jump was, but it wasn't an axel," Myra snapped. "Next time spring up—pop that takeoff. You're making such simple mistakes, Kirsten. You almost tripped over your blades when you changed feet on that combination spin."

I stared down at the ice, afraid that if I looked at Myra, I'd burst into tears. Suddenly a brilliant idea struck me. "I'm not feeling very well," I began. "My throat is all scratchy. I hope I'm not coming down with the flu that's going around my school."

"All right. That's enough for today, then. If you're not going to give it your all, I'm not going to stick around and waste my time. Go home and gargle—get your mother to make some chicken soup," Myra said. "You don't have time to be sick right now."

It worked! Sure, I felt a bit uneasy. I didn't like to lie. But as I got into my car my heart hammered in my chest. I never thought it could be so simple. I'd get a convenient short flu and call in sick on Saturday. Then I'd be able to watch Troy's game and he couldn't be mad at me. What harm could be done? After all, I'd never skipped a practice before.

Friday morning I appeared at the rink without any makeup, and I wore my black leotard and wool tights . . . and of course my gray gloves. I never skated without my gloves—my hands would freeze without them. Black always made my pale complexion look washed out when I didn't wear blush.

"Did you drink chicken soup like I told you?" Myra glared at me critically.

I nodded. "But it doesn't seem to be helping too much. My throat is better, but my head feels so heavy today."

All through practice I skated like someone who was about to be deathly sick.

"I like the way you are moving in the slow section of your routine today, Kirsten," Myra called to me. "Light and wispy. That's good. Remember to keep that feeling."

I did a quick turn and began skating backward, crossing one foot over the other. Then I went into a camel spin. I made a small circle with more backward crossovers around the center of the rink. I stepped into the spin with my left foot, whipping my body around quickly, gaining speed and momentum. Raising my right leg, I arched my back and pulled both arms back so my body was one fluid line.

After about ten rotations, the wind blowing in my brown ponytail, I lowered my right leg and brought my foot quickly in toward my left knee. I pulled my arms in hard and at the same time moved my right foot straight down toward the ice. This rapid movement gave me the power to turn very, very fast before I finished with a perfect scratch spin.

"Now that's how I expect you to skate," Myra cheered. "I guess that soup helped more than you thought. I think you're ready to land that triple today," she said. "It's about time you got it. We can't do any serious work on the routine if you keep falling or doubling it."

"How are you feeling?" Myra asked as I showed up for afternoon practice that day.

"Not too great," I whined, pulling a tissue out from my left sleeve. I always kept a tissue there when I had a runny nose. It was the truth this time. Maybe it was the power of suggestion, but I didn't really feel very well. "But I plan to get that triple jump today. You promised we'd work on it."

"Good girl," Myra said. "Let's do it."

I finished my warm-ups, gliding around the rink with ease, then started my approach for the jump. Why was the triple so impossible? I could turn easily around twice in the air. I just needed a little more speed to be able to spin around once more. It was all in my mind. If I could visualize it, I knew I could do it.

I went into the jump and fell. I tried it again and fell again. I was getting madder and madder at myself. And it was hard to concentrate with all those other skaters watching me, especially the ones who giggled and pointed every time I fell down. The rink was surprisingly crowded for a Friday afternoon. And that just made me more miserable.

"What's wrong with me?" I demanded. "Why can't I do it? How did you prepare for triples when you used to compete, Myra?"

Myra shook her head. "Me? I could never do a triple jump."

"Never?" Myra was pretty old, probably in her forties or fifties, but she'd been a champion once.

She smiled. "In my day only men did triples, and only very few men too. Doubles were considered very daring."

I felt as if I were about to snap. "So you're trying to teach me something you've never even done?"

"I'm a coach," she explained. "I know enough to teach you how to do it."

"But I need someone to *show* me," I cried. I looked around the rink. In the crowd of skaters there was no one for me to look up to. No one to watch . . . to learn from. Usually I liked being the star, the best at the rink. But suddenly I felt completely alone. "I'm never going to get it."

Myra stared out into space, thinking. "Maybe I should take you over to Coach Vladimir in San Mateo. He has skaters who can do a triple. And he's coached Russian Olympians—solos and pairs. As a matter of fact, Vlad is one of the world's experts on pairs coaching."

I knew all about Coach Vladimir. I'd seen him working with his skaters at competitions, and he was kind of scary. He was a huge bear of a man, and he yelled and waved his arms a lot. Coach Vladimir was an old Russian guy who had come to America a couple of years ago. He had been a top-ranked coach in the Soviet Union. I was sure he could help me with my jumps.

I swallowed hard. "Okay, let's try him," I said, looking around the rink again. Some of the beginners were staring at me. "I'm certainly not going to learn it here, with all these brats watching me."

"You are in a bad mood today," Myra said, shaking her head.

I coughed, remembering Troy and my phony illness. "Maybe it's that flu."

"Make sure you go straight to bed when you get home tonight," Myra soothed.

She seemed unusually concerned about me. And her worried look made me feel totally guilty. Myra was my coach. She cared about me. How could I deceive her? But there was no turning back now. I wanted to be there for Troy.

I felt terrible the entire drive home. It was more than guilt. I felt as if I might really wake up with the flu in the morning.

Saturday I woke with only a headache. I'd had terrible dreams all night long. Something to do with being on a football field that was made of ice, trying to catch a ball and falling down, with everyone laughing. Boy, was my conscience playing tricks with me. Was it worth it? Should I suffer so just to make Troy happy? Did his game really mean that much?

I wasn't the kind of person who liked to let other people down, and now I was stuck—either way I'd let somebody down, either Troy or Myra.

I waited until about nine-thirty before I called Myra. I prayed that she wouldn't be there, that I could leave my message on her answering machine. But it wasn't my lucky day.

"Hello, Myra Richards," she answered.

"Myra?" My voice sounded weak and frail as it cracked. "It's Kirsten and I feel terrible." I groaned. That wasn't a lie. I did feel terrible, about what I was doing. "I think I should stay in bed and try to shake this off."

"You've never canceled a practice before, Kirsten. Is something else going on here?" Myra asked. She sounded suspicious.

"No, really, Myra. I just feel lousy. You know I wouldn't miss a practice unless I was *really* sick." Boy, this was harder than I thought it would be. But I couldn't give in. Not now. I was so close to being with Troy. I had to make Myra believe.

"I see. Well, I certainly can't make you do something you don't want to do. I don't agree with you, Kirsten, but if it must be, it must be. I'll see you on Monday, then."

My mom walked past my door just as I hung up.

"Who was on the phone, dear?" she asked.

"Myra. Just, uh . . . an idea I had for the routine."

"But you'll be seeing her in a couple of hours." She came in and perched on the end of my bed.

22

"It couldn't wait," I said.

"Is everything okay at the rink? I haven't had a chance to watch you since you got your own car."

"It's okay." I pulled the covers up over my body. "I'm still having problems with the triple toe loop. Myra's taking me over to San Mateo . . . to work with Coach Vladimir. His skaters can do triples. I need to be around strong skaters, and there are only beginners at my rink."

My mom was supernice. She'd driven me twice a day, every day, until I'd learned to drive, and she'd never once complained. My parents weren't rich, and skating had cost a lot of money. I knew they'd gone without vacations and new cars so that I could skate.

Mom got to her feet again. "I must come and watch you soon. I haven't even seen this new routine you're working on. Are you going to be working on it today?"

Alarm bells went off in my head. "Not today!" I said a little too loudly. "Saturdays are always so crowded, so we'll just be working on figures—boring stuff like that. That's what we always do on Saturdays." Mom couldn't show up today.

She smiled. "I don't have too much time today anyway. I have to drive your brother to a soccer game in an hour. But don't think I've lost interest in your skating just because you're old enough to drive yourself."

I threw the covers off, stood up, and wrapped

my arms around her neck. "You're a great mother, you know that?" I said. "I'm going to nominate you for mother of the year. In fact, when I win the Olympics, I'll skate over and present my medal to you!"

"You crazy nut," she said, laughing, but her face was pink, as if she were pleased.

As soon as she'd left, the guilt feelings came back, twice as strongly. My lies were growing by the minute. First I'd lied to Myra and then to my mom. But there was nothing I could do about it now. I'd get that triple once I began working with Coach Vlad. Then today's missed practice wouldn't matter, would it?

The game was fantastic. Troy played like he'd never played before. He threw long touchdown passes, and the crowd went wild. Everyone jumped up and down, screaming Troy's name. I cheered too . . . until I thought about Myra. What was I doing there? What if today was the day I had been destined to land the triple toe loop? What if I'd never land it?

"We did it!" Troy announced as he found me after the game. He ran a hand through his longish brown hair. It was damp with sweat, and his cheeks were still rosy from exertion. "We won the game and it's all thanks to you, Kirsten! You see, I knew you'd bring me luck." He put his arm around my shoulders. He smelled of sweat and grass. "Let's go celebrate. I'm starving."

"Are you going for pizza?" one of the other guys called out to Troy.

"Pizza? I want to celebrate with something special," Troy said. "Let's go to Spengler's Fish Grotto. I feel like splurging on my beautiful girl-friend. My good-luck charm."

I felt better by the second. This was definitely worth missing one practice. I'd spend some quality time with Troy, maybe cuddle a little on the ride home, and be fresh for a new week of jumps and spins by Monday.

A whole group of us crammed into Troy's car and drove down toward the Bay. We got a great table at the Fish Grotto and had a really delicious meal—an enormous plate piled high with fried fish and clams and scallops and shrimps. I felt relaxed and happy. Until I glanced up at the door. Myra.

At first I thought I was hallucinating, that my mind had conjured her up. But she was real, all right. I quickly ducked under the table, as if I were picking up my napkin. Then I peeked cautiously as Myra was led to a table across the restaurant from us.

I nudged Troy under the table. "Myra's here. I've got to get out of here before she sees me. Meet me outside."

Without waiting for an answer, I ran blindly for the door. I stood in the bright California sun-light, trying to stop my panicked heart from pounding. I felt as if the world were about to open up and swallow me whole.

Troy joined me almost immediately.

"Do you think she saw me?" I asked, peering back at the door as if she might appear any second.

Troy grinned at my worried face. "Hey, relax," he said, his arm around my shoulders. "It's not like you're wanted for murder. So you skipped a practice. Big deal. You need some time off or you'll burn out."

"You just don't understand, Troy. You don't understand anything, do you?" I pulled out from under his arm, a tear running down my left cheek.

He didn't say anything for a minute or two. Then finally, "You know, Kirsten, it's great to be dedicated. I'm dedicated to football. I want to get to the top, but I want a life too. I manage to find a way to hang out . . . have some free time for my friends. For you. But you don't have a minute for anything but skating."

Troy just didn't get it. This was my only chance at fame. If I didn't make the next Olympics, I wouldn't get another opportunity. Troy had years before he had to play serious football. The pros didn't begin until after college. If I didn't make it now, I'd lose everything I'd worked so hard to achieve.

THREE

"MYRA, WHAT A nice surprise," I heard my father say as I helped my mother put away groceries that night in the kitchen. "Please, come in."

I had been waiting for Myra to call and tell me that she'd seen me at the restaurant . . . that she knew I'd lied to her. Now my heart almost stopped beating. I looked around the kitchen for a way to escape, my brain desperately trying to come up with a good excuse.

Dad brought Myra through to the kitchen. "Look who's dropped in for a chat."

My mother pulled out a chair. "Myra, sit down. Can I get you anything? A cup of tea or coffee?"

Myra's face was like a mask. I couldn't read her expression. "Thank you, no. I'm glad to find you all home. There's something important I'd like to discuss with you. It's about Kirsten's future."

I held my breath, trying to pretend I was invisible. My parents sat at the kitchen table opposite Myra, looking at her expectantly. I pulled out a chair and sat, staring at the pattern on the vinyl floor.

"As you probably know," Myra continued, clearing her throat. "Kirsten has been having problems with her triple toe loop. I'm sure you realize she needs at least one triple if she is to medal at the next Nationals." She paused.

Just tell them already! I wanted to scream. *Tell them I lied to you and skipped practice today.* The tension was killing me.

But instead she went on, "I have been doing some serious thinking and I've come to a decision. I no longer think that I am the best person to coach Kirsten."

I looked up then and met Myra's gaze. "But Myra . . . ," I began. She held up her hand for me to be quiet.

"I told Kirsten about Coach Vladimir in San Mateo. I believe he can help her with her jumps. He was one of the top Russian coaches before he came here a few years ago. This has not been an easy decision for me, but I think Coach Vladimir is who Kirsten needs right now. She has outgrown me."

"But Myra, you've done wonderful things for Kirsten," my mother said. "She looks up to you. You work so well together."

Myra was still staring at me, as if she could see

into my mind. "I do not think Kirsten believes I can teach her any longer. She feels she has outgrown me. Isn't that right, Kirsten?"

"No, that's not true, Myra," I said. I felt I might cry any second.

Her face relaxed. "Kirsten needs more than I can give her. She needs the competition and stimulation of other skaters at her level. She needs a coach who will push her to her limits. I have been too soft with her."

Too soft? If she was soft, I was afraid to see what hard was.

"If Kirsten really wants to make it to the top, she will need total dedication from now on," Myra said. "No distractions, no slacking off . . . no boyfriends." Her gaze never left my eyes.

Did she know? She must have seen me at the Fish Grotto. This was her way of punishing me.

"Coach Vladimir has coached Olympians before," she continued. "And he has other skaters at her level. That's what Kirsten needs right now."

My parents just looked at each other, then at me.

"If you really think that's best for her . . . ," my father started.

"I do," Myra said. "I would like to arrange a meeting between you and Coach Vladimir as soon as possible. Kirsten's training should not be interrupted. I'd like her to begin next week." She got to her feet. "Talk it over and call me."

Myra turned toward me, a sad smile on her face. "I've enjoyed working with you all these years, watching you blossom into a lovely young skater. But I don't want to hold you back. I really do want what's best for you, Kirsten. I hope you do too."

I nodded. I knew that if I opened my mouth to speak, tears would come pouring down my face. However nice Myra was acting, it was obvious to me that she didn't want to work with me anymore. I was being politely dumped by my coach.

I had never felt so happy and so sad at the same time. I felt as if I were closing a door on my old life—and stepping into a whole new world.

My parents and I discussed the switch, and I changed my mind about Myra dumping me. Working with Coach Vladimir was the best idea. I was excited about working with an Olympic coach . . . a coach who had other advanced skaters. So my father called Myra, and she arranged a meeting with the new coach at the rink in San Mateo, forty-five minutes away from home, on Monday evening.

I was nervous and excited at the same time as we drove to San Mateo. I'd have a top-level coach and maybe even some friends at the rink, something I'd never had.

The San Mateo rink was medium size and brightly lit. There were locker rooms directly across from the main lobby. Down a long hallway were a snack bar and a weight room. Loud dance music blared from the speakers as an ice-dance couple practiced their routine. There were a bunch of younger girls working with a female coach off to one side, and little boys in helmets seemed to be waiting for an ice-hockey practice.

Coach Vladimir was waiting for us in one of the bleacher seats beside the rink. He stood up when he saw us and held out his hand. "So this is the little lady who wants to learn the triple jump, huh?" He had a big, deep, rumbling voice to go with his huge, bearlike appearance. Coach Vladimir took my hand and almost crushed it.

Up close he was even bigger and fiercer looking than I had remembered. I had to stop myself from telling him I'd made a mistake and running straight back to Myra.

I nodded shyly and managed a smile. He shook hands with my parents and offered them a seat.

"I've seen you skate," he said in a strong Russian accent. "You move well. Last year at Junior Nationals—what did you place?"

"Eleventh," I admitted. "That's why I need your help with my jumps. Myra can't seem to teach me the triple toe loop. I was hoping you could."

"That is why you are switching coaches?" he asked, staring down at me with his bright blue eyes.

"That and other things," I explained. "It's too lonely for me over at Berkeley. I'm the only advanced teenager there. All the other skaters are beginners . . . little kids."

He nodded as if he understood. "It is true that you work better with peers around you. You need friends so that you can gripe about the mean old coach, huh?"

He grinned, and I smiled back. Maybe he was human after all.

"And you need rivals to push you to be better," he finished. "I think it's a good idea. If you come to work out here, you'll make my other skaters work harder. Yes. I am happy."

At that moment I noticed a light-haired guy as he skated onto the ice. He looked more confident than any other guy skater I knew. He was wearing old gray sweatpants with a stretched-out black turtleneck that made his light eyes and straight light brown hair glow. This guy was big for a skater. In fact, he looked as if he belonged on the football team with Troy. And he was definitely as hot as Troy—hotter maybe. He looked like a Swedish skier, with his blond-streaked hair and tanned skin. He skated smoothly around the ice, gathering speed with each step he took. He was as graceful as a wild animal—like an antelope or a gazelle. I couldn't take my eyes off him. Then suddenly he took off into an impossibly high jump. It was only a single axel, one and a half rotations in the air from a forward takeoff. And he didn't hold his arms quite right. But he was so high that he seemed to hang there, suspended in midair. It was as if gravity had no effect on him. Sometimes I jumped like that in my dreams, but never in real life.

"Who's that?" I blurted out before I could stop myself.

"That is my newest skater, Kai Bergstrom," Vlad said, sounding pleased with himself. "He has only been doing figures for six months. Not bad, huh?"

"He's only been skating for six months?" My mother sounded astonished.

"Only been *figure* skating for six months." Vlad beamed. "He's been skating all his life. He was a top hockey player."

"That's weird," I said, keeping my eyes on Kai. I'd never seen anyone move so fast on the ice before. I felt the rush of cold air as he skated past us. "No one switches from hockey to figure skating."

"Kai had some sort of accident," Vlad explained. "He asked me to work with him to keep him in shape."

Kai had passed us again, this time skating backward, crossing one foot over the other. He gathered speed and prepared for another impossibly high jump. "There doesn't seem to be too much wrong with him," I said. "What kind of accident was it?"

"I can't be sure. Kai has never talked about it," Vlad said. "He is not what you would call a talkative young man. In fact, he is not the easiest person I have coached. What a temper, but what raw talent! It makes me excited to think of how far he can go if he puts his mind to it."

"Hey, Coach," Kai yelled from the middle of the rink. "That jump was better, wasn't it?"

Kai's eyes seemed to sweep right over me. He was completely focused on Vladimir.

"Much better," Vlad called. "Now work on the arm position. Remember what the ballet teacher showed you?"

Kai made a face. "That sissy stuff? Give me a break, Coach. Do I look like the kind of guy who dances *Swan Lake*?"

"I tell you where your arms should go. If you wish to be my student, you just do what I say!" Vlad yelled, his voice no longer gentle.

Kai looked at the coach as if he were about to argue, then shrugged and moved away. "You're the boss," he said. "I guess I'm through for the day anyway."

I watched Kai skate to the edge of the ice. He stepped off in one easy motion, striding out for the locker room without looking back.

"Kirsten?" I felt my mother's touch on my arm and realized that I hadn't heard a word anyone had said.

"I'm sorry," I said, feeling myself blushing.

"Coach Vladimir wants to know if you would like to start in the morning," she said.

"Or do you need longer to talk it over at home?" Vladimir asked.

"I don't think we need to talk it over," my father said. "If this is best for Kirsten, then it's up to her to make the decision."

"I'll be here in the morning," I said, a huge smile across my excited face. "What time?"

"Six o'clock sharp. And I don't tolerate lateness."

My mother nudged me. "I'm glad you're driving yourself now. You'll have to get up half an hour earlier. It's a longer commute."

I hadn't thought of that before. She was right—the longer commute would take another huge bite out of my already precious free time. Now I'd see Troy even less often. I'd have to find a way to make it work.

When I got home, I called Troy.

"So did Myra chew you out for missing practice?" he asked.

"No, she didn't say anything about that. But she feels I need a new coach. Someone who's trained top-level skaters before. He's a Russian called Coach Vladimir."

"A Russian guy, huh? I don't know if I like you spending all your time with another guy. Maybe I should show up at your new rink and check him out."

I laughed. "He's old and fat, and he has gray hair. He looks like a grouchy Santa Claus." I shifted my cordless phone from my right ear to my left. "He used to coach Russian Olympians."

"Russian Olympians, huh? Sounds cool," he said. "You should go for it, Kirsten."

"Coach Vlad has other skaters at my level, which will be good for me." I rolled over onto my stomach. I was lounging on my bed—my favorite place to talk to Troy. "They'll make me work harder." As I said this, a picture of Kai flashed into my mind. I saw it all again—the incredible speed, the impossibly high jump, and the defiant look in his eye as he told the coach he wasn't about to dance *Swan Lake*.

"Other skaters? That will be good," Troy said. "It will be more fun for you."

I blushed, determined to stop talking about the other skaters. I didn't want Troy to know about Kai . . . that he was built like a Greek god.

The next morning I staggered out of bed when my alarm went off at five, grabbed my skating bag and the breakfast bar and protein shake I had put out the night before, then headed for the long drive to San Mateo. At least the freeways weren't crowded at that early hour. It wouldn't be so much fun in the afternoon.

The new rink looked kind of spooky when I entered. It wasn't fully daylight outside and only a couple of the overhead lights had been turned on, leaving the high ceiling in shadow. In the total silence the slightest sound echoed. I could even hear my own breathing. I could see it too—smoke coming from my mouth like a dragon's breath.

It felt cold—colder than my old rink in Berkeley. And I was sure my outfit wasn't helping me fight the morning chill. I had wanted to look good on my first day at the new rink. So I had put on my purple wool tights, leggings, and matching leotard, but I hadn't added the usual big sweater and gloves I usually wore for warmth.

I shivered as I stood clutching my skates, feeling the coldness of the blades digging into my palms. I wasn't making a big mistake, was I? I hoped Vladimir wasn't as tough as I had heard and that the other skaters were friendly.

I sat on one of the front benches, slipping my feet into my stiff leather boots. I had brought my fairly new pair, again, wanting to look my best. Bending over, I quickly began to lace my skates. I glanced sideways as a girl sat on the bench next to me. She began putting on her own skates.

I thought I had seen the girl on the ice before. If she was who I thought she was, I knew she was a beautiful skater with a very dramatic presence. Her moves were smooth and lyrical.

She had big, dark eyes and thick black hair swept up into a ponytail. She wore a totally spectacular outfit, a red sweater, matching skirt, and leggings. I'd seen it in a skating catalog, and I knew it was way too expensive for me. As she got closer, she stopped and did a double take. So did I.

"Kirsten Hayes? Is that you?"

I leaped to my feet. "Alice Attwood? I thought it was you. What are you doing here? I thought you lived in southern California."

"We moved up here so I could train with Vlad," Alice explained, beaming at me. "What are you doing here?"

"I switched coaches. I'm training with him too."

"Are you serious? That's incredible." She grabbed my hands. "Kirsten, this is so great! Finally I have a friend to skate with."

I was pretty excited too. "I know how you feel. I had nobody to talk to at my old rink. It was so boring skating alone."

Alice sat down beside me and started taking off the white skate guards she wore to protect her skate blades while walking on the padded floor that surrounded the ice. "Why did you leave your old coach?"

"I have to learn the triple jump or I'll never have a shot at medaling at the Senior Nationals. My old coach couldn't seem to teach it to me."

She nodded. "Triples are so hard. It took me a while to get the flip and the toe loop, and I still can't get the triple lutz yet."

I shot her a quick look as she took off her other skate guard. She could already do triple flips and toe loops? Suddenly I felt scared. I was used to being queen of the rink. Now I'd be number two—or worse, if there were better skaters than Alice.

I laced up my second boot, tying it in a double knot, and looked at her again. Alice wasn't any better than I was. We'd competed against each other before. I'd even beaten her in Providence last year. Alice must have learned the triple since she'd started working with Coach Vladimir. That was a good sign. Once Vlad started coaching me, I knew I'd be flying through the air too, doing triple flips and toe loops and even axels! All right, I knew only a few women in the world had ever completed a triple axel in competition, but I could dream, couldn't I?

I finished lacing my skates and got to my feet. "What's he like?" I whispered as I saw Coach Vlad heading in our direction.

"Vlad? He's okay," Alice said. "He makes us work pretty hard. Try stopping for a second to breathe and you're in trouble. Sometimes he gets in a bad mood, but he can be funny too. He tells terrible jokes—you know, the kind that second-graders tell?"

"I know all of them," I said. "My younger brother used to own every joke book there was. He drove us crazy with his knock-knock jokes for years. Thank goodness he's grown out of that stage now."

"You have a brother?" Alice asked, sounding as if I'd announced I had a pet elephant. "You're so lucky. I hate being an only child. My parents fuss over me all the time," Alice admitted as she stood up. "If I said I hated a teacher, my mom would have her fired."

"That wouldn't be so bad," I said, laughing. "I can think of plenty of teachers I'd like to have fired."

"And if I said I liked a boy, she'd call him her-self and set us up on a date," Alice went on. "Well, maybe not a date. Not if it interfered with skating. Skating has to come first in my life."

"Yeah, I guess it has to. But it can be a pain sometimes. My boyfriend doesn't understand. He thinks I should be at all his football games, even though he knows I have to practice."

"You have a boyfriend?" Alice looked at me enviously.

I grinned. "Yeah. He's the quarterback at school. He's so cute."

"I don't have time to meet guys. I don't have time for anything except skating. I wish I could write for the school newspaper, but they meet after school, so that's out. And now my mom's talking about getting a tutor for me so that I don't have to go to school at all."

"A tutor? Wow, that'll cost megabucks."

"They don't mind," Alice said. "My dad's a lawyer, and my mom has nothing else to do except follow my skating. She hated when my dad gave me a car for my sixteenth birthday and she couldn't drive me to the rink anymore."

"She hated it?" I exclaimed. "My mom couldn't wait for me to drive myself. She's so happy that she can sleep past five o'clock now."

"My mother still drops by to watch me all the time," Alice said. "She always makes some ex-cuse, like I left my hair scrunchie behind or she's brought me some hot chocolate." She gave me a frustrated look. "You can't miss her. She stands right next to the barrier and waves to me. A fat lady in a dark mink jacket who calls out instructions to the coach. She is so embarrassing. I beg her not to come, but she doesn't listen."

"Uh-oh. We'd better get onto the ice," I said. "Here comes the coach."

"Yeah, he doesn't like it when we sit around," Alice agreed.

"So how many other skaters does he work with?" I asked as we headed for the ice.

"Just me and a couple of guys." Alice moved closer to me as we glided out onto the ice together. "I'm really glad you're here, Kirsten. I hate working out alone, and you know what guys are like. They think they're so superior . . . especially Mr. Macho."

"Do you mean Kai Bergstrom?" I asked.

"You know Kai?"

"I saw him yesterday. Coach told us about him. What a hunk, huh?"

"I admit he looks great, but I'd stay away from him if I were you," Alice muttered. "Kai's not exactly Mr. Congeniality. Talk about an attitude problem! He totally thinks he's better than everyone here, even though he's just started skating figures."

"Will you girls stop yakking and get to work?" Coach Vladimir's voice boomed across the rink. "If you're going to whisper together instead of work, then I'll have one of you come to practice

41

at four in the morning, all alone. And you won't want to be around me at four in the morning. I'll be in a very bad mood. And when I'm in a bad mood, everybody suffers. Understand me?"

"Don't worry," Alice whispered to me. "He says stuff like that all the time. But he doesn't really mean it." We exchanged grins.

Coach Vladimir frowned at us. "Quit talking and start working, Attwood," he growled. "And you too, Kirsten. I want to see what Myra has taught you. Get warmed up and let's take a look at those jumps you're having such trouble with."

Alice took off and I followed. I did my stretches at the edge of the ice, then I skated out after Alice. I built up speed, crossed to an inside edge, and went into a big inside eight, which I always found very satisfying. I think it had something to do with making the two large circles intersect perfectly in the middle.

This is great, I thought, glancing across at Alice as I completed one circle and struck out into the second. I watched as she moved past me, doing backward crossovers in preparation for a jump.

I finished the figure eight and went into some dance steps and then into a layback spin, which was something else I did well. I watched as Alice landed a beautiful double toe loop. Now I was determined to show Coach Vlad what I could do.

I picked up speed. What would impress him most? I didn't want to risk doing something I might miss, landing on my butt my first time here. So I decided to play it safe with the double toe loop. I could do that in my sleep—maybe even better than Alice had just done.

I dug in my edges and went faster and faster. Cold air stung my face and snatched at my breath. I could hear the crisp swish of my skates as they cut into the fresh ice. I felt my ponytail streaming out behind me. The rink barrier flashed past in a gray blur. I loved that feeling of speed and power.

I looked back and had positioned my arms in preparation for the jump when suddenly I noticed a large, dark shape at the edge of my vision. It was heading toward me at an amazing speed. I swerved, almost fell, and fought to keep my balance. I managed to right myself at the last second as I screeched to a stop and spun around angrily.

It was Kai, the Nordic hunk. He came to a halt a few feet away, sending up a shower of ice with his blades, the way hockey players did.

"Watch where you're going!" he yelled. "Get off the ice. This is a private practice session." His eyes shot cold, blue fire at me.

I fought hard to keep my cool. "I know it's a private practice session!" I yelled back. "You don't think I'd be here at six in the morning if I didn't have to be, do you? I'm Coach Vladimir's newest student."

Kai looked surprised, but it only stopped him for a second. "Then you'd better learn to keep out of my way," Kai warned.

"Maybe you should learn to keep out of my way," I said smoothly, "because I'm going to the Olympics."

He gave a little half smirk. "Not if you keep skating into other people like that, you're not."

I gave him my frostiest stare. "Obviously you're new to this, or you'd have seen me getting a medal when I was only fourteen." I was about to mention Nationals too, but I stopped myself. Eleventh wasn't something I wanted to brag about. Besides, the way Kai looked at me, his eyes half mocking, half challenging, made it hard to think clearly. How could a guy be so gorgeous and so obnoxious at the same time?

He gave a mock bow. "Well, excuse me," he said. "I guess I'd better not take up any more of your precious practice time then. Just watch where you're going, huh?"

"Ditto," I said. "For your information, we're not playing hockey here. The goal is *not* to collide with people."

FOUR

IT TOOK ME a couple of weeks to get used to my new routine—if anyone could ever really get used to staggering out of the house at five-fifteen in the morning and drinking a cold protein shake on the way to the rink. I used to be able to pop home after morning practice, change my clothes, and still have time for a quick breakfast. But not anymore. Now I barely had time to grab a tasteless granola bar on the way to first period.

That meant I was starving by midmorning. I was on a very strict, healthy skater's diet. Those skintight costumes didn't allow for one extra pound. But Berkeley High's cafeteria salad wasn't only disgusting, it didn't fill me up at all. And then after school I had to head directly back to San Mateo again for an hour of ballet twice a week and an hour in the gym with a trainer on the other afternoons. All before two more hours on the ice. By the time I got home every night, I was exhausted and ready to eat a horse!

I tried to be good, to eat only my protein bar on the way to afternoon sessions. But most afternoons I was so famished that I couldn't walk past the rink's snack bar without grabbing a quick bite.

One day, the second week I was there, I went on a major binge. I bought two jelly doughnuts and a giant hot dog with the works. Turning to carry my snack to a table, I felt an annoying tap on my shoulder.

"Skater's diet, huh?" Kai asked sarcastically. "Weren't you there for the trainer's lecture about junk food yesterday?"

"For your information, I leave home at five-fifteen every morning. I haven't had more than a couple of lousy protein bars and a salad for the past week," I snapped. "Give me a break, Kai. I'm starved!"

"Oooh, you do have a tough life, don't you, ice princess?" he teased. "Where do you think the rest of us have been—at Denny's? I leave my house even earlier than you do every morning. I come all the way from San Jose. I guess guys just have more willpower." He stepped up to the counter. "I'll just have an herb tea and a yogurt . . . make it nonfat," he said to the girl behind the snack counter.

The pretty brunette glanced at me, then at Kai. "Are you sure you don't want one of those sticky buns you had yesterday?" she asked sweetly.

46

"Ha!" I laughed. "Guys have more willpower. Yeah, right."

Kai almost looked as if he might laugh. But then he shrugged. "Actually, it doesn't matter if I put on any extra weight. I'm not planning to enter competitions."

"You're not?" Why would anyone work so hard if they weren't going to compete? "Then why are you here? Why get up so early and work your butt off every day?"

He gave me his standard smirking smile. "Let's face it. Figure skating is for losers. You don't see any *real* guys here, do you? I'm just skating to stay in shape." Then he turned and marched out of the snack area. He didn't even wait for his yogurt.

The brunette behind the counter shook her head. "You never know where you are with that guy. One day he's real sweet, the world's biggest flirt. Next day he'll bite your head off. I'd stay clear of him if I were you."

"That's the best advice I've heard all day," I muttered.

Most nights I got home feeling as if I'd just been through the world's longest day. I barely had the strength to eat dinner, and I usually fell asleep doing my homework. Even if I was home early enough to catch a late movie, I was too pooped to party.

At first Troy thought my new coach was a

great idea. I'd even overheard him boasting to a friend at school that now I had an Olympic coach, big stuff. But one day it must have dawned on him that San Mateo was an extra forty-five minutes away. That I wouldn't have the energy to see him during the week.

"Where were you last night?" Troy asked at lunchtime Thursday afternoon, draping an arm around my shoulders. "I called around seven and your mom said you weren't home yet."

"Where do you think I was? Skating," I snapped. My schedule was making me cranky. I certainly didn't need any hassles from Troy on top of my exhaustion. "It's a long drive from San Mateo."

"I never get to talk to you, Kirsten," Troy whined. "You don't have time for me anymore."

"I don't have a choice," I said, stabbing at a soggy piece of tasteless lettuce. I didn't blame Troy for being frustrated with my new schedule, but he wasn't making it any easier on me.

"You really have to work with this Vlad guy, huh?" he asked as he scarfed down his second peanut butter sandwich. "Maybe Myra wasn't so bad after all. At least I got to see you when she was your coach."

"What do you want me to do?" I asked with a laugh, trying to lighten the conversation. "Blow my chance to work with the best coach in the area, if not the world, just because he's an extra half hour away?"

"No, of course not," Troy said quickly, chugging a gulp of soda. "It's just that . . . well, I just miss you, Kirsten. We hardly got to spend any time together before . . . when you worked with Myra here in Berkeley. And now we have even less time to be together."

"I know. And I'm sorry, Troy. I wish there were a way I could do both . . . work with Coach Vlad and be with you every afternoon. But I can't do it. This is how it's got to be right now." I surrendered to the salad, tossing my fork onto the tray.

When he didn't say anything, I went on. "C'mon, Troy. You're an athlete. You know what it's like. If the coach at a top school offered you a scholarship, under the condition that you worked an extra five hours a day, you'd do it, wouldn't you? And you'd expect me to understand."

"I guess," he said slowly. "But it's hard, Kirsten. I mean, what's the point of having a girl-friend if she's never around?"

"I'm around Saturday nights," I said. "And I'll try to make it to all your Friday-night football games. Just the weeknights are out. And you don't get out of football practice until five anyway during the week."

"But what if I want to go out after practice? Spend some time with my favorite girl?" he asked, sounding like a hurt little boy. He finished his sandwich and opened a bag of chips.

"I can't believe you. You don't actually expect me to quit skating . . . give up my shot at the gold just in case you want to do something one night?" I was trying to be reasonable, but I was getting madder by the minute.

"Sure, why not?" he said, but he laughed this time. Then he leaned across and kissed my nose. "It's okay, Kirsten. I know you have to do this right now. I don't suppose it's easy on you either. I'll try to be a warm and sensitive guy, try to understand your feelings, okay?"

"Yeah, right!" I said, smiling. "You? Warm and sensitive?" I snuggled closer to him on the cafeteria bench. I wanted to make all my bad feelings go away . . . lose myself in Troy's rugged, soapy smell.

"Hey, I can be as warm and sensitive as the next guy if I want to."

I knew Troy really cared about me. That was why he wanted to spend more time together. He was a great guy—and my key to popularity at Berkeley. I didn't want to lose him. But I wouldn't stop skating for him. Somehow I'd gotten myself into this situation. And somehow I'd find a way to make it work.

Vlad had worked me really hard those first few weeks. He even had me go back to the basics. We went over my every approach, takeoff, and head position. Yet each time I thought I'd gotten the jump set in my head, my body wouldn't comply.

Vlad thought it might be helpful to work on my spins. Do something I was good at—something I was confident about—then move on to jumps.

50

"What would you like to see first?" I asked Friday afternoon.

"Let's try a back camel spin."

I glided to the center of the ice, did several backward crossovers, and then transferred my weight to my left foot. I swung my right leg around in the air and leaned forward, carefully keeping my back arched and my chin up. Then I spun on the ball of my left foot. I made sure I kept my arms straight out on both sides of me . . . concentrating on keeping the same pace throughout the spin. Perfect. I couldn't wait to show Vlad another turn.

"Good. Now let's see your sit spin," Vlad called out next.

I went into my sit spin, one of my favorite spins. Building up speed, I lowered my body into a sitting position, held my arms out in front of me, and spun on my left foot, extending my right leg. I was feeling really good now.

"Great!" Vlad cheered. "Now we are going to watch Alice demonstrate a triple jump. Just watch first, Kirsten, then copy exactly what she does."

Talk about humiliation. Why was Alice able to get the triple when I couldn't? And why didn't Vlad let me try one myself before making me watch Alice show off?

Alice must have seen how miserable I was after she demonstrated her jumps because she followed me to the edge of the rink when the Zamboni drove onto the ice. That was the tractorlike machine that cleaned the ice. All the skaters had to leave the ice before the Zamboni could get to work.

Alice stood beside me as I flopped onto a bench.

"I don't see why I can't get it," I growled to her.

"It'll come, don't worry," she said kindly, sitting beside me. "It takes a while to get used to a new coach. Maybe you're just tired from the long commute."

"You're right," I said. "I'm totally exhausted. And it's not just the fact that I have to get up early and drive all the way here. I'm stressed out about Troy."

"Is he giving you a hard time?" Alice asked, wiping some ice off her blades.

"No. Yes. Well . . . he's trying to be understanding," I explained, "but I know he's bummed about being the only guy on the team whose girlfriend can't go out for pizza after practice. I know girls are always hanging around him. I don't want to lose him, Alice, but I'm not going to stop skating to be with him."

"I only wish I had your problems."

"There's always Kai," I teased.

We both turned to look at Kai on the ice. The ice looked brand-new, sparkling as if thousands of diamonds had been crushed under the weight of the mighty Zamboni. It was the afternoon practice session, so we didn't have the rink to ourselves. Vlad's students had to share the ice with other kids getting private lessons. And there were always people watching us from the snack-bar windows or arriving early for the next public skate.

Kai skated over to the barrier and began talking to a group of girls, who gazed up at him adoringly. Kai seemed to be totally hamming it up as if he loved being the center of attention.

"At least Kai's not afraid of girls," she said.

"If Kai was a nicer person, I'd help you get together with him," I said. "You two would make a cute couple."

I watched as Kai waved to his fans and skated back out onto the rink. Finding an empty patch of ice, Kai created a circle by doing backward crossovers. Then he leaned and stepped with the outside edge of his left skate blade into the center of the circle. I knew he was about to attempt a sit spin.

I was hypnotized by his raw, masculine strength as he whipped his right leg around while bending his left knee in one fluid motion. Kai squatted very low to the ground. He was supposed to bring his head down and put his arms out gracefully in front of his outstretched leg, all the while controlling the rapid spinning motion. But he didn't. Kai was probably too busy concentrating on completing the thirteen required revolutions for the sit spin to be correct.

My heart pounded in excitement as I watched his power. Kai might be a royal jerk, but boy, could he skate!

Then, keeping his weight on his left skate, Kai stood on one leg and pulled his right leg around rapidly. He ended triumphantly to the roar of his gushing fans in the stands.

I couldn't believe how quickly Kai had progressed. His form was getting better, especially when he stayed far away from me.

Since our collision Kai and I had hardly exchanged two words. In fact, I'd made it a point to steer clear of him. I had enough stress in my life without trading insults with a loser like him.

I stepped onto the ice, ready to get back to my jumps. I had to focus, blot everything from my mind except that triple. Blot out Kai's strong legs and muscular shoulders. *It's all up to me,* I reminded myself. *If I want to nail the triple, I just have to visualize it.* But every time I landed on my rear—and that meant every time I attempted the triple—there was Kai, smirking at me and ready with a rude comment.

"Going to the Olympics, huh?" he muttered as he skated past me. "What as—a hot-dog vendor?"

I glared at him, wiping ice off my butt. "I haven't noticed you doing a triple jump yet."

"It's doubles this week," he said smugly. "Triples are next week. Quads will be the week after."

"In your dreams."

"My dreams are much more interesting than that," he quipped, raising an eyebrow.

I felt myself blushing, which made him grin even more. Kai seemed to be getting a big kick out of making me feel uncomfortable. Well, I'd show him. I couldn't wait until I nailed that darned jump. That would finally wipe Kai's slimy grin off his perfectly chiseled face.

I suppose you could say that having Kai around made me work even harder. He certainly brought out a side of me I never knew I had before. I'd always thought of myself as kind of shy around guys. But Kai seemed to push all the wrong buttons with me.

"So what's his problem?" I asked Alice later that day. We were taking a quick break.

"His problem?" Alice asked.

"Kai's certainly cute enough," I said, watching him fool around with another girl on the bleachers. He was sitting under a group of flags from various countries that hung above the seats around the rink. "But his attitude stinks. Why is he so hostile?"

"I suppose it's that whole hockey thing. You know, since he had to drop out of the league," she explained. "I heard he was a great player—good enough to have a scholarship and make the pros."

"So why's he doing figures?" I asked, skating in a circle around Alice. "Is it really just to keep in shape?"

"I guess," she said, her eyes following him as he left the girl and stepped onto the ice. He picked up speed, prepared to jump, and leaped into the air with tremendous strength and grace.

"He looks like he's ready to go back right now. If he can jump like that, I'm sure he could play hockey."

"Maybe he likes figure skating better than hockey now," Alice suggested.

Just then Kai came flying past us, sending up a shower of ice in our faces. "Maybe he's decided he can't tear himself away from the two cutest skaters in California," I whispered.

Alice giggled as Kai glanced our way.

Kai went into a simple spin, tripped, and fell facedown. He slammed his fist onto the ice. "Why can't I get this stupid thing!" I heard him yell, his voice echoing around the rink. He looked over at Alice and me. "What are you staring at, huh?" he growled.

"Just reminding ourselves how *not* to do a spin," I called to him. I wasn't going to let him get the better of me this time. And as he rose to his feet I licked my finger and indicated that I'd just scored a point. I thought I saw a hint of a grin as he skated away.

"Kirsten? Alice? Are you two already so perfect that you don't have to work?" Vlad called out.

We quickly moved to the center of the ice. "Just taking a breather, Coach," I said.

"That's enough breathing. Time to get to work," Vlad growled. "And Kirsten, I need to talk to you in my office after practice," he added.

Alice shot me a look. "Why does he want to talk to you and not me?"

"Maybe he's decided that I'm going to skip Nationals and go straight to the Olympics," I said lightly.

"But you can't even do the triple jump yet," Alice said nervously.

"Just kidding, Alice," I said. "Lighten up. Maybe he's going to tell me I'm a bad influence on you, that I make you giggle too much."

Alice smiled, then and skated away. "Enjoy your talk with Vlad," she called out.

Later that afternoon I entered Vlad's office overlooking the rink. Glancing around the room, I noticed every inch was filled with skating stuff. Trophies, warm-up clothes, posters, skating bags, clumps of broken laces . . .

"Sit down, Kirsten," Vlad said, pointing to a chair.

I sat. The chair was one of those small, uncomfortable wooden fold-up chairs.

Vlad looked at me. "Kirsten, I'm afraid I'm going to say something you might not like to hear. I've been watching you since you arrived here, and I've noticed something. Something that will change your entire life. Kirsten, dear, I don't think you're going to master that triple toe loop."

"You mean not in time to put it in my routine for Nationals this year?"

"Not ever. At least, not in the foreseeable future."

It was as if time stood still. I felt as if I were a balloon that had just been pricked. All the air was rushing out of me. There was no sound except for the Zamboni machine, creeping its way around the rink to put a new surface on the ice.

"But I've almost got it. Give me another week or so. . . ."

He shook his head. "I just don't think you have the leg strength. I don't think you ever will."

57

"But Alice can do it. And I beat her last year."

"Alice is built differently than you," he explained. "She's more muscular, less curvy. It doesn't make her a better skater . . ."

"No, just one who can do triple jumps when I can't," I finished for him.

He nodded. "But you have qualities she doesn't have." He leaned on his desk. "You have a real feeling for the music. You relate well to the ice. There is emotion in your skating."

"Sounds like I've got a great future in the chorus line of the Ice Capades," I said bitterly. "You know I'll never make it to the Olympics without the triple."

"Maybe, maybe not," he said mysteriously.

"What do you mean?"

He leaned toward me even more, as if he were about to whisper a secret. "As a solo performer, you don't have what it takes, Kirsten. And I doubt that will change as you mature. But there is something special in your skating that is worth pursuing. You have qualities that can take you to the very top. So maybe we should look in another direction."

"What direction?" Now that Vlad had just told me I'd never make it to the Olympics, I wasn't sure I could bear hearing his "solution."

"I'd like to see how you work with a partner. I think you could be a first-class pairs skater."

"Pairs skating?" I didn't want to be a pairs skater.

He nodded. "That is my specialty. With all modesty, I can tell you that I am one of the world's experts in pairs skating. Ever since I came to America, I have been looking for a couple to train in pairs. I'd like to make you into a world-class pairs skater."

"But who would be my partner?" I asked.

"I can find you a perfect partner. That's no problem," Vlad explained. "I'd like you to go home and talk this over with your parents. Give it time. Think about it. It's a very big decision."

I stared hopelessly out the window, watching the Zamboni go around and around like a large beetle. That was how I felt—like a trapped insect hopelessly going around and around and desperately trying to find the way out.

"What choice do I have?" I said at last. "You just told me I'll never make it as a solo skater."

"I didn't say never," Coach Vlad cut in. "I know of skaters who have come to their peak in their twenties."

"I can't afford to wait that long," I said. "It's now or never, Coach. I want it so badly right now. Who knows how long that feeling will last? I have to get to the Olympics any way I can. If you say that pairs skating is my only chance, then I guess I have to take it."

He nodded. "I don't think you'll regret this, Kirsten," he said, leaning back in his chair now. "You're a natural for pairs skating. As I said, you skate with such emotion. The judges look for emotion in pairs more than in solo skating. Now, for the perfect partner I promised you . . ."

"You have someone in mind?" I asked.

Vlad got up, went to the door, and opened it. "Would you come in now, please?" he called.

My mouth dropped open as Kai strolled into Vlad's office, taller and more overwhelming off the ice than on. He stood there, looking as confused and defiant as I felt.

"Kai, remember our little talk?" Vlad began. "I'd like you to meet your new partner."

Kai's ice blue eyes looked down into mine. "Her?" he said at exactly the same moment I said, "Him?"

FIVE

KAI LOOKED AT me as if I were a bad smell under his nose. "You can't seriously expect me to skate with her, Coach," he said. "She's an ice princess . . . thinks she's better than me because she's been doing figures all her life."

"Ice princess! C'mon, Vlad, you're not really suggesting I skate with him? Kai's just a beginner!" I stood up and pointed at Kai.

"See what I mean, Vlad?" Kai demanded. "Listen, sweetie, I can outskate you any day." We were facing each other now.

"Prove it, beginner. Put your skates where your mouth is!"

"I wouldn't want to get in Her Highness's way. You need all the space you can get to fall on your flabby butt." I turned away and stared out the window, trying to ignore Kai's rude words. "Seems you spend more time sitting on the ice than skating these days."

61

I couldn't take much more of his abuse. "Maybe it's because I've been practicing triple jumps, something you'll never master. And my butt's not flabby," I snapped.

We stood there, glaring at each other like two angry dogs who'd just met on the street and were preparing to attack.

Vlad stepped between us. "Please, please," he begged. "There is no need for this childish behavior. You have to learn to get along if you plan to work as a team."

"Listen, I never *planned* to take this figure skating seriously." Kai stepped back. "You were the one who said I had talent, that I should try it out. But I have to be honest, Vlad, figure skating is for losers."

"Losers!"

"Well, maybe it's okay for girls," Kai amended. "But guys don't figure skate—not real guys. They do stuff like football and hockey."

"Then why don't you go back to hockey and leave us in peace?" I sat back in the uncomfortable chair in front of Vlad's desk. "I'm sure your bad temper and attitude fit right in there."

A strange look passed across Kai's face. Panic? Sadness? Fear? His emotions seemed almost palpable . . . yet not quite within reach. Gone was the arrogant guy who seemed to enjoy making me suffer. Suddenly Kai looked vulnerable. "I can't go back to hockey yet," Kai said, hesitating. "I'm only here to get back in shape, just in case . . ."

"You work on a pairs routine with me and you'll be in shape for anything, young man," Vlad promised, guiding Kai to the chair next to mine. "I intend to work you both until you drop and beg for mercy. And if you stick to it, I think you'll find you can compete against the best. Come on, give it a try."

"Well, I have nothing to lose right now," Kai said, shrugging. "But don't expect me to stick around forever. And I don't know about the competing thing."

Vlad looked at me. "Are you willing to give it a try, Kirsten? I'm not asking you to make a final decision today. Let's just work together and see if it's right for both of you. If you decide you want to go back to solo work, you'll have lost nothing. You might even learn some new moves."

I looked at Kai, then back at Vlad. "Okay," I said slowly. "I'm willing to give it a try. But if Kai thinks he can put me down all the time, I'm out of here right now."

Vlad clapped and smiled. "Good. Then it is settled. Tomorrow I enter your names in the Pacific Coast Sectionals."

"Sectionals?" I blurted. "But Coach, that's less than two months away. We'll never be ready in time."

Vlad shrugged, sitting in his chair again. "If you're not ready, then we scratch. No harm done. But I think we must work as if we intend to win this competition. Then we can go on to

Nationals in February. We begin tomorrow—Saturday—at five-thirty. I have arranged for us to be alone on the ice through the afternoon. Be prepared to work very hard."

And with that, Vlad led us out the door.

So there I was, standing outside Vlad's office, feeling as if the entire world had just closed in on me. The weight of Vlad's words quickly crashed down on me with the sound of his door slamming shut. I wouldn't be going to the Olympics—not as a solo skater. No more Kirsten Hayes . . . future Olympic star. Vlad had thrown out everything I'd worked so hard to achieve with a few painful words. My skating career was a washout . . . just like me.

"Hey, are you okay?" Kai interrupted my thoughts. "Kirsten, you seem upset. I didn't mean to hurt your feelings in there. It's just that . . ."

"Don't be ridiculous." We had left Vlad's office and were walking down the rubber matting toward the rink. "I can accept this switch . . . and the fact that I'll never land a triple toe loop," I lied.

I didn't think I'd ever be able to deal with that. But I certainly wasn't going to tell Kai my true feelings. He'd just make it a joke and upset me more.

"Well, just for the record, I think this is a crazy idea," Kai said. "It'll never work. I don't know why I let Vlad talk me into it. I'm only here to get back in shape, not to compete."

"You seem in pretty good shape to me," I said, taking in his long legs and strong shoulders.

"There doesn't seem to be much wrong with the way you move on the ice."

"Glad you noticed," Kai quipped, then he stopped grinning as I glared at him.

"What's the deal with hockey? Why can't you go back?"

"It's a long story," he snapped. "I don't want to talk about it."

"I'm sorry I asked."

We continued silently down the hallway, side by side. I was very conscious of Kai towering over me as he walked beside me.

"What I don't understand," Kai began after a while, "is why *you're* doing this. I mean, isn't it better to get to the Olympics as a solo performer? You seem the type who wants the limelight all to yourself."

"Vlad just told me I won't get to the Olympics as a solo skater," I said flatly. "I can't do the triple toe loop. My legs aren't strong enough. And Coach doesn't think I'll ever nail it. So I can't follow my real dream anymore—just like you can't follow your hockey dreams. And like you . . . I don't want to talk about it. I just want to go home."

He looked at me as if he were seeing me for the first time. "So we're both failures, then. Maybe we really do belong together."

"Speak for yourself," I said. "I don't consider myself a failure. I'm just changing directions, that's all. I intend to get to the Olympics by any means necessary."

*   *   *

What have I done now? I asked myself as I parked my car in the driveway at home that night. *I've just agreed to work out for five hours a day with the skating partner from hell. I must be out of my mind.* But something had made me do it, and it wasn't Kai's muscular chest or even his great smile. It was the way he had looked for just a fraction of a second when I had asked him why he didn't go back to hockey. It was as if I'd peeled off one of his layers and seen the frightened little boy underneath.

I didn't know the whole story, but I got the feeling that something major had happened on that hockey rink, something that Kai was afraid to face. I wondered if that was why he acted like a big shot now, to deny some deep-down fear.

So maybe we did have something in common. Because I was afraid too. I was afraid of failing, of finding that Troy had been right. Of finding out that I'd put in all those years of hard work and skating for nothing.

I haven't really committed to anything, I reminded myself. *I just said I'd give it a try.* I could go back to singles if I wanted. But I didn't know what I wanted anymore. . . .

I took a deep breath before I opened the car door . . . before I slowly walked to the front door and entered my house. I knew I had to tell my parents about quitting singles . . . about skating with Kai. But I also knew that I'd have to seem positive or they'd see how upset I really was. I just wanted to tell them and run to my room. I needed a chance to deal with this on my own. Alone.

"Mom, Dad, are you home?" I called as I entered the house. "I need to talk to you both." I found them in the kitchen and told them the news.

They looked at me as if I'd told them I wanted to take up skydiving instead of pairs skating.

"Pairs? Why?" my father asked.

"Is this something you'd want to do?" Mom jumped in.

"Vlad says I'm not strong enough . . . I'll never be strong enough to medal as a solo skater. He thinks I've got a better chance of making it to the top with a partner," I explained, fighting the tears that threatened to fall. This was harder than I'd thought it would be. "And he's one of the best pairs coaches in the world. I said I'd give it a try. If I find it's not for me, I can always go back to singles."

My parents spent the next half hour grilling me about my decision. They just wanted to be sure I was making the right move . . . that Vlad hadn't bullied me into doing something I wasn't interested in. After a few tears—mine, not theirs—and lots of hugs, my parents and I were able to accept me as a pairs skater. They helped me understand that this was a good thing. That Vlad wasn't insulting me. He just wanted me to get what I deserved. And I knew I deserved a chance at the gold . . . by any means possible.

Before I had a chance to go to my room, the phone rang. *Now what?* I thought.

My dad answered it. "Kirsten, it's for you. It's Troy."

Troy. With my life falling apart around me, Troy was the last person on my mind.

I dashed up the stairs and ran down the hall to my room. Tossing my skate bag on my bed, I picked up the cordless and called down to my dad, "I've got it, Dad." Then I waited to hear the click on the extension downstairs.

"Hi, Troy," I said, cradling the phone on my shoulder. I flopped down on my bed, kicked off my shoes, and leaned back against the cuddly brown bear Troy had given me on our third date.

"So what's new?" Troy asked.

This was the perfect opportunity for me to tell Troy about skating with Kai. But suddenly I found that I didn't want to. *No sense in telling him about it right now,* I told myself. *Not before I'm totally sure that this is what I want to do.*

"Just the usual." Then I filled him in on everything that had happened that day . . . everything except the fact that I'd be skating with a totally gorgeous, totally rude guy for the next two months. As I talked I felt happy for the first time that day. Troy's deep, familiar voice soothed me and I was able to forget all about Kai and his never-ending dimples.

Troy cleared his throat. "I, uh . . . called because I wondered . . . you know. . . . Well, tomorrow afternoon . . . ," he coughed this time. "I know you've got to practice in the morning, but it's a really big game. And you said your Saturdays are pretty free."

But before I could tell him I had to practice all day instead of just a few hours in the morning, the phone clicked. Call waiting. "Hold on a minute, Troy. I've got another call."

I pressed the button. "Hello?"

"Hi, Kirsten?" a strangely familiar male voice said over the phone.

"Yeah, this is Kirsten." I couldn't quite place the voice. "Who is this?"

"It's Kai."

Why was Kai calling me? Didn't I see enough of him at the rink?

"I wanted to talk to you about this pairs thing. Do you have a minute?"

"Uh, sure," I said. I was sure whatever he had to say wouldn't take long. But Kai and I talked for about twenty minutes. Kai told me that he was afraid we were making a big mistake. He didn't want to lead me on, make me believe he wanted to go all the way to the competitive level. I told him what my parents had said . . . that we should take it one day at a time. I wasn't sure myself of how I felt about skating with Kai. It was all too new. We had a real heart-to-heart, and by the end of the call I felt a little closer to Kai.

"Thanks for the talk, Kirsten. Guess I'll see you tomorrow on the ice."

I hung up feeling better about skating than I had all day. I rolled over onto my stomach and . . .

Troy! I had totally forgotten about Troy. I quickly grabbed the phone and pressed the receiver button. Nothing. No Troy on the other end. Just an angry dial tone. I had left him on hold the entire time I'd spoken with Kai.

"What can I do now?" I cried, looking up at the digital clock on my white dresser. 10:15. It was too late to call Troy back.

I sat up, my head in my hands. I'd have to figure out a way to make it up to Troy, to tell him that I hadn't meant to leave him on hold. But even worse, how was I going to explain why I couldn't make it to tomorrow's game?

SIX

KAI WAS ALREADY on the ice when I came out early Saturday morning. He was wearing his usual black turtleneck, which made his light brown hair glow like a golden halo. He looked good, very good. I wondered if Kai's muscular build and perfect smile would be an asset. Maybe all the female judges would give us perfect scores. . . . I grinned to myself. Maybe this pairs thing wasn't such a bad idea after all.

"Do you think you're too good to show up on time?" Kai demanded as I took off my skate guards at the edge of the ice.

What happened to the nice guy on the phone last night? Kai was like Dr. Jekyll and Mr. Hyde. Friendly one minute and a monster the next.

"I drove all the way from Berkeley. I can't always judge what the traffic is going to be like on the bridge." I finished lacing up my boots and put on my favorite gray gloves.

71

He looked surprised then. "So why don't you just skate at the rink in Berkeley?"

"Because Vlad coaches here. Is that a good enough reason for you?"

"I've got a long trip too," he said, skating toward me. "I drive up from San Jose."

"Don't the Sharks play hockey at the San Jose arena?" I stepped onto the ice and skated in a small circle.

"I like it better here," he said quickly. "C'mon, let's warm up." Kai changed the subject. "I want to get started on this pairs thing. I can't wait to learn how to lift you high up in the air."

I hadn't really thought about lifts. Sure, I knew they were a major part of pairs skating, but I hadn't thought about what it would be like to be lifted in Kai's strong arms. A picture flashed through my mind—Kai's muscular arms around my thin waist . . . me floating higher and higher, my face close to his . . .

He'll probably drop me on purpose, I thought.

Vlad tottered over to us. Vlad never wore skates. His usual outfit consisted of worn-out brown pants, a waist-length tan jacket, and an old pair of sneakers. The sneakers were probably the reason he walked so strangely across the ice. "That's enough, you two. Let's begin." He clapped us to attention. "Remember, this is a professional partnership. You don't have to like each other. You just have to work together. Understood?"

72

We both nodded.

"First you must get the feel of skating as a team. Each partner must be a mirror image of the other. Two hands moving as one. Two legs lifted just so, as if you are both puppets moving to the same set of strings, okay? Kirsten, take off your gloves."

"Do I have to, Coach? My hands get so cold."

Vlad shook his head. "You can't work together with gloves on. You need to know what your partner is feeling."

"Right now I think she's feeling that she doesn't want to work with me," Kai said.

Unwillingly I took off my gloves. I always wore gloves when I skated. That way my hands wouldn't freeze when I fell onto the ice.

"Now join hands and skate around the rink," Vlad instructed. "Adjust your steps so that you move together."

Awkwardly Kai took my hand. I felt a strange sensation tingle through my arm as his strong, warm fingers clasped mine. Kai's hand was softer and larger than Troy's—the only other hand I could compare it to. My heart began to race at his touch. I wasn't sure whether I was excited or scared or embarrassed. I tried to concentrate on skating. Left foot, right foot, left foot . . . *This is a professional partnership, Kirsten. Nothing else,* I reminded myself.

Then Kai took off with giant strides.

"Hey, wait up," I yelled, trying to catch up to him. "I can't go that fast."

"Then learn to speed up."

"I don't have long legs like you. You'll have to slow down." Why was it that every time I began to feel warmly toward Kai, he had to open his mouth and ruin the moment?

"But you move as slow as a snail." Then he turned and stuck out his tongue at me.

"Quit mumbling and start working together," Coach called. "Left and right and left and right." He clapped as he spoke. We obeyed, and suddenly we were skating together.

"Now put your arm around her waist," Vlad called. "Keep on moving. Same pace, left and right and crossovers on the corners . . ."

Kai's arm came around me, holding me tightly. And suddenly we were flying around the ice. I'd never experienced such speed before. My skates barely touched the ice as we rounded the corners. *This is like magic,* I thought. *This is the way I skate in my dreams.* My eyes were shining with excitement. I never wanted to slow down.

But Vlad called for us to stop. "You seemed to get the hang of that pretty easily," he said, nodding with satisfaction. "You move well together. It's a good start."

"Once she got up to my speed, it was fine." Kai had to add his two cents, of course. That brought me back down to earth. I had almost forgotten that my dream partner also happened to be a major pain in the butt.

"Now let's practice a little waltz. The waltz turn

74

is used a lot in pairs skating to change the position of the couple. You know the waltz steps, no?"

"Sure," I said, at the same time as Kai said, "I don't."

"You never learned the waltz steps?" I asked, delighted to be one up on him. "It's so easy. Just three turns over and over."

"I've only been doing this six months," he snapped. "And believe me, when I played hockey, we didn't waltz too often."

"Show him, Kirsten. He'll pick it up quickly," Vlad said just as Alice skated up to us in her fancy lavender skating dress. A row of sequins along the collar sparkled under the rink's fluorescent lights.

I can't believe she's wearing such an expensive dress for practice, I thought with a twinge of annoyance. My own best skating outfit was nowhere near as fancy, and I only wore it for competitions. My white wool tights and long brown sweater looked like rags next to Alice's outfit.

"Can you watch my triple lutz now, Coach?" she interrupted. "I think I've almost gotten it."

I had the feeling she was a little jealous when I told her that morning that Kai and I would be skating together. Now it seemed like she was butting in just to impress us.

"All right, Alice. Show me your lutz," Vlad said calmly. "These two have to learn the waltz step."

"The waltz? I learned that when I was six," Alice said, shooting me a challenging look. "I could teach them if you want."

"I know how to do the waltz, Alice. Kai needs to learn, and that's only because he started figure skating six months ago," I explained. "He'll pick it up quickly when I teach him."

A current of tension sparked between Alice and me. Suddenly I felt as if this weren't about skating the waltz at all. It was about Kai. Alice seemed to need to prove to Kai that she was the better skater. That she could do the jumps I'd never master.

I shot her a nasty look, then turned to Kai.

"Yoo-hoo, Alice, darling," came a high-pitched voice from the side of the rink. "You left your box of tissues at home and I know you've had the sniffles."

"Oh, no. Not my mother!" I heard Alice mutter.

Alice's mother was determined to see her succeed as a figure skater. I knew she wanted Alice to have every advantage, and she put lots of pressure on Alice to win. Ms. Attwood attended almost every practice and was always ready to criticize Alice's performance.

"Okay, Alice. You have my full attention," Vlad said. "And now your mother is here to see you do your triple lutz too."

"Yes, Alice, honey, show me what you've learned this week," her mother called.

"I've changed my mind, Coach," Alice said, her head hanging down in defeat. "I think I'll work on figures." She skated to the far side of the rink.

Kai raised an eyebrow as he leaned toward me.

"Aren't you glad you don't have a mother like that?" he whispered.

"Alice hates when her mother comes here," I agreed.

"'Show me what you've learned,'" he mocked. "Give me a break!"

His eyes were laughing into mine, as if we were sharing a silent joke. Kai looked different when he smiled. His dimpled face lit up, and his eyes crinkled adorably at the sides.

We spent the rest of the day working on the waltz. It was strange, but by the end of the session I began to enjoy sharing practice with someone else. I never realized how lonely solo skating was—just you and a yelling coach. But pairs skating was somehow intimate. Just you and your partner against the world. Sure, we still had to deal with a screaming coach, but somehow it was easier with a partner on your side.

Where is he? I had been looking for Troy since Saturday afternoon. After Coach Vlad had sent us home, I drove straight to the football field at school. I thought I might catch the last touchdown or something. But I was too late. The field looked like a ghost town. You never would have known that there had been a game just a few hours before.

I drove home after that and called Troy's house. But no one answered. I didn't want to leave a message on the answering machine. Troy probably wouldn't have called me back after I'd left him on hold the night before. I called all day Sunday too, but again no one answered.

Now it was Monday afternoon, and I hadn't run into Troy all day. It was as if he had simply vanished. He was probably avoiding me on purpose.

I walked toward my locker, my head hanging low. Suddenly I looked up. Troy was a few people ahead of me. "Troy!" I called down the crowded hallway. He looked good in his worn blue jeans and his Berkeley High football jacket. *This is your only chance to apologize, Kirsten. Don't blow it now.*

Troy looked up. He didn't seem happy to see me.

I took a deep breath and walked toward him. "I've been looking for you all day," I said. I couldn't make myself look him straight in his chocolate brown eyes.

"Really?" Troy sounded as if he didn't care if I were alive.

He wasn't going to let this be easy. "About the other night. I'm sorry I left you on hold." I adjusted the backpack on my shoulder and prayed for Troy to speak.

"Yeah, well . . ."

"But I didn't have a choice," I lied. I realized that this would be the worst time to tell Troy the truth. To tell him that I was speaking to another guy instead of him. I couldn't tell him about Kai, not yet. Not until I was completely sure about the pairs thing myself. "My dad got an important call—that's who beeped in on us. And then it was too late to call you back."

The first warning bell rang. "Whatever." Troy groaned. "Listen, I don't want to be late for bio. Catch you later."

"But Troy. We need to talk. . . ." But he just continued walking toward his next class. I let out the breath I didn't know I'd been holding. Now what was I going to do?

SEVEN

THE REST OF that week Vlad worked us so hard that I didn't have the time or energy to worry about Troy. The Pacific Coast Sectionals were less than a month and a half away, and Kai and I had barely passed square one. It didn't matter that we both knew how to spin or jump or turn. Now we had to do those things together, without hitting each other as we swung our arms and legs.

Everything went smoothly those next few days—as smoothly as anything could go with Kai around—until we tried to select music for our two routines. In pairs competitions you had to perform a short program, which had several required lifts, spins, and jumps, and a long program, which was your free skate. And both of them had to be performed with the perfect music to bring out the mood you hoped to create.

"I'm not skating to any kind of flowery stuff like

that," Kai demanded when Vlad played a beautiful piece by Rachmaninoff. Personally, I liked the music. "Can't we skate to something with a pounding beat? Something written in this century?"

"Well, I'm not skating to Snoop Doggy Dogg," I said.

Kai laughed. "Hey, maybe we could start a trend. You know, wear gang colors and bandannas for costumes . . ."

"No. It doesn't have to be classical music," Vlad explained. "But it must express a range of emotions. Let's listen to some show tapes and see if there's something we can work with."

We settled on a song from *Phantom of the Opera* for our free skate and then Vlad found a bizarre piece of electronic music that we all agreed on for our short program. Vlad thought we could have a robot theme, and the routine could tell the story of two robots coming to life through love.

Kai spluttered at this. "Coming to life through love! Give me a break."

Vlad smiled knowingly. "You've got a lot to learn, young man."

Wednesday, Vlad showed us the opening of the free skate program he was creating for us. We began in a pose in the center of the ice, then took off at full speed into side-by-side double flips. A double flip was a backward takeoff from our toe picks, with two full revolutions in the air. Then we joined up for a waltz sequence until we were in the center of the ice again for side-by-side spins. These were required elements.

For the spins Vlad wanted us to do flying camels. The flying camel was similar to a camel spin—the only difference was the approach to the spin. With the flying camel you had to perform a high-flying leap onto your spinning leg. Using the momentum from the leap to propel the spin, you had to raise one leg arabesque style, all the while picking up speed and centering your body. This move was a bit complicated, and Kai couldn't seem to get it.

"We'll have to change it, Vlad," I said after we'd botched our fourth attempt at doing it. "Kai can't do a flying camel."

"I can too," Kai said. "You keep swinging your leg out too far. You're always in my way, Kirsten."

"I am not. I have one of the best flying camels in the business."

"Hey, I've got a better one," he said.

"Prove it!"

"Watch me." He pulled up the back of his dark gray sweater to make a hump and then flapped his arms. "Flying camel, see?"

"Will you stop fooling around," I demanded, rolling my head on my shoulders. I had to keep the tension from building in my neck. "We have to get this right."

"Lighten up, Kirsten," Kai said. "Why do you have to take everything so seriously?"

"Because it's important. We have less than two months before the competition. I don't want to look like a fool out there, even if you do."

"There are other competitions, Kirsten. The world won't come to an end if we don't make this one."

"It will for me."

He shrugged, skating away from me.

"Don't flake out on me now, Kai," I warned.

Kai continued moving to the center of the ice. I watched as he practiced the flying camel on his own.

Kai tried harder after that. We learned more and more of the routine, and then it was time for our first lift. The press lift.

Vlad started us off in the gym, working out on thick rubber mats so I wouldn't get hurt when Kai dropped me.

Vlad showed Kai exactly where on my legs to put his hands and then had him lift me. Kai started to lift, then groaned and put me down again.

"I only weigh a hundred and three pounds," I said indignantly.

"It feels like two hundred and ten," Kai said, leaning over and rubbing his back. "You have to help, you know."

"Yes, Kirsten. He's right," Vlad said. "You can't just stand there like a deadweight. You must leap into the lift. Let the force of your leap help carry you upward. Now try again."

"Like this?" Kai asked.

I went flying upward until I was suspended

83

over Kai's light brown head. "Whoa!" I yelled, grabbing his soft hair as I felt myself falling.

"Hey, let go of my hair! It feels like you're pulling it out," Kai yelled.

"I'll fall if I let go!"

"You won't fall. I've got you. Trust me."

I let go, Kai's arms buckled, and I landed in a heap on the mat.

"That's the last time I trust you when you tell me to let go," I complained, brushing myself off as I stood up again.

"I guess I should have realized that your head is the heaviest part of you," Kai quipped, starting to laugh. "It sure is swelled enough."

"Ha. Ha. Very funny. Maybe you should work out with weights before we try this again—build up some muscle in those puny little arms."

"Maybe you should eat less breakfast so you don't weigh as much."

"Save your energy, please," Vlad said, clapping us to attention. "Now, once again."

After an hour of practice in the gym that day, Kai had lifted and dropped me at least a hundred times. My hipbones felt totally bruised and sore, and Kai was rubbing his tired arm muscles.

"You see, Kai," Vlad said cheerfully. "I told you that pairs skating would give you a complete workout."

"I think I'd rather be in the weight room," Kai said, glancing at me with a grin. "Barbells don't complain when you drop them."

*   *   *

"Drop me and die," I whispered to Kai as we skated out together Thursday morning.

Kai chuckled as if he thought I were funny. Didn't he take anything seriously?

This time it was even scarier because Kai was about to lift me on the ice. I pushed off with my skating leg and went into the preparation for the press lift. I helped Kai with a good push off the ice. His strong hands lifted me as if I weighed nothing at all. Suddenly I was flying out above the ice. Afraid, I tried not to look down. But I couldn't help myself. The ice looked so far away and very, very hard. I remembered how painful it had felt when I'd landed on a soft mat. I didn't want to know what it would feel like to fall so far onto the ice.

Just as I started thinking those thoughts, Kai got off balance and I felt myself slipping.

"Whoa!" I yelled, grabbing onto Kai as I felt myself falling. I wound up with my arms around his neck, his hands holding me, our faces inches apart.

"See, I knew it. You can't resist me. You're just like all the other girls," Kai teased, but he didn't let me go.

"In your dreams," I snapped. Suddenly I was very conscious of his strong arms around me, of his heart beating against mine. I wasn't prepared for the way he was making me feel. "Please let me down," I said in my coldest voice.

"Gladly. You know, most girls would give anything to be in my arms."

"I guess I must be the only girl with good taste, then. And in case you get any other crazy ideas, I think you should know that I have a boyfriend. He's the star quarterback at Berkeley High."

"Well, isn't that special," Kai teased. "But don't worry. I wasn't getting any ideas. Lifting you is like lifting weights at the gym—only heavier, and not as much fun," he cracked.

Why do I bother? I thought. *Kai's the most conceited, obnoxious guy I've ever met.*

But I didn't want to quit either, because Kai definitely had something. His skating was still a bit wild and uncontrolled, but people stopped to watch him . . . to watch us. And it wasn't only the girls who drooled over his strong chest and arms, his chiseled good looks. If we could get our act together—correction, if Kai could get *his* act together—we'd make those judges sit up and take notice. It was worth putting up with Kai and his attitude to see if we really could learn to be a pair.

In addition to working on the ice and in the gym, Vlad insisted we spend more time with our ballet teacher. Most of the lift positions in skating were actually ballet lifts, and I had to learn to be raised and lowered gracefully. This certainly helped our skating, but it made our workouts even longer.

"This is crazy," Troy said Friday afternoon. We were in the hallway outside my history classroom. I hadn't seen Troy since our awkward conversation on Monday. "I feel like I haven't seen you in weeks." Troy leaned down and kissed my nose. Where was the passion we used to have? Maybe we were just getting too used to each other.

"I saw you at my locker on Monday, remember?" I was trying to keep it light.

"You know what I mean. And hey, sorry I got so mad about that call-waiting thing." Troy reached out and held my hand.

I had been right. Kai's hands were bigger, softer, and warmer than Troy's callused hands. Troy was so physical, handling me like I was one of his teammates. He wasn't nearly as gentle as Kai—even on Kai's worst day. I stopped myself, suddenly realizing that I was comparing my boyfriend to Godzilla.

"I guess I've been a little on edge recently," Troy continued. "But between the play-offs coming up and never getting to see you, I'm going crazy." He paused, moved even closer to me, then went on. "At least I don't have to worry about you talking to other guys while I'm playing my guts out." He laughed.

I tried to laugh too, but my heart did a flip-flop. I still hadn't told Troy about Kai. And the longer I waited, the harder it became. I knew it was wrong, but I couldn't risk a big scene. I was so tired of fighting with Kai that I just wanted things to be simple with Troy. And it was much easier if Troy didn't find out that I was skating with the best-looking pairs skater in the country. I'd tell him the truth soon, just not yet.

Suddenly the warning bell rang. "Please tell me you'll be at the play-off game tonight."

"I'll try."

"It doesn't start until seven-thirty." He was already running down the hall.

"Then I'll be there," I promised.

Later that afternoon Kai and I started out with the simple spins and lifts, gradually progressing to more complicated maneuvers.

"Okay. Let's try the throw jump you've been working on," Vlad said.

"I don't know about this," I muttered to Kai. We had gotten it okay when there was a soft mat waiting for me to fall on in the gym. But I wasn't so sure about being thrown through the air and having to land on one thin blade on the cold, hard ice.

"Don't worry," Kai said. For a second I thought he was about to say something nice to me, but then he went on, "I'll try to tame my incredible strength. I don't want to throw you so high, you get hooked up in the fluorescent lights."

"You are so funny," I said, scowling at his grinning face.

"Hey, calm down, Kirsten," he whispered. "It's going to be just fine."

We started to skate together, moving at the same speed across the huge rink. Everything became a blur as Kai lifted me into a straight arm lift and turned with me above his head. Then he gently lowered me until I was in front of him.

"Now!" Vlad called with a loud clap.

Suddenly I was flying into the air as Kai threw me. It was such a massive throw that for a second I felt as if I were hanging weightless in midair. The next thing I knew, I landed hard on the ice. I could feel the bruises already forming on my legs.

Kai burst out laughing. "Nice landing," he called.

I got to my feet, my eyes shooting daggers at him. "That's it! I've had enough!" I yelled, skating toward the side of the rink.

"Come back," Kai called. "I'm sorry. I didn't mean to laugh."

"I bet you didn't."

"I didn't. I swear." Kai came speeding toward me. "You just looked so funny, flying gracefully through the air, and suddenly *splat*."

I glared at him. Then I turned to Vlad. "I'm not working with him anymore, Coach. I almost broke my tailbone and he thinks it's funny. You said this was just a trial period. Well, I've tried and it's not working. Either find me another partner, or I'm going back to solo skating."

EIGHT

"**D**ON'T BE A baby, Kirsten." Vlad came over to me, his arms open wide. "You're both tired. It's the end of the week and you've been working very hard. Kai meant no harm."

"Oh, no," I said. "I'll bet this was the highlight of his week. Too bad I didn't land on my head— that probably would have made him even happier."

"That probably would have cracked the ice," Kai teased as he skated circles around me. "You're the most hardheaded person I know."

"Ha, ha."

"Enough of this," Vlad said, so fiercely that we both shut up instantly. "Why don't you put all that energy and emotion into your skating? I tell you what. We have practiced the moves hundreds of times. Now let's try them with the music. You will skate the first part of your new routine for me."

"But we don't really know it yet," Kai interrupted.

Vlad held up his hand. "You will do your best. When you skate to the music, I think you will see things quite differently. It won't seem like hard work anymore. Take your position for the opening, please." He tottered across the ice in his old sneakers and put a tape in the recorder.

Kai and I took up our pose in the center of the ice. My rear was still smarting from that fall, and I was so angry with Kai that I could hardly think straight. I didn't know how Vlad expected me to concentrate on our routine.

As the first organ notes of the *Phantom* music echoed out across the ice, we started to skate side by side, faster and faster. The beat of the music picked up until the bass throbbed and swept over us. Then the strangest thing happened. Suddenly I wasn't conscious of skating at all.

The music had turned Kai and me into one creature with four arms and four legs. I couldn't even tell if it was my arm touching Kai or his arm touching me, lifting me. I didn't have to look to keep in sync with him. It was as if I were inside his head and I could feel what he was thinking.

I floated up into the press lift and then sank down gently to the ice again. I felt Kai's heart thumping against mine, pounding to the beat of the music as he held me, as the powerful chords flowed over us. And I forgot completely that this was the world's most obnoxious guy, that we didn't even like each other.

It was wonderful and scary at the same time.

The moment the music ended I looked at Kai and could tell he had felt the same way.

"Wow!" he said. "That was spooky."

Vlad ran out to us, clapping like a little kid. "See, I knew it!" he cheered. "I knew I was right. I can tell chemistry when I see it."

"Chemistry?" The only chemistry there had been between me and Kai until now had definitely been acid. So how had Vlad guessed that we'd skate together so well?

I could sense Kai looking at me, and I slowly raised my eyes to meet his.

"See," he whispered, his warm breath tickling my ear. His eyes teased mine. "I can do a flying camel when I need to."

"You sure can," I agreed, trying to catch my own breath.

"We were pretty good out there, weren't we?" I nodded.

"Maybe this figure-skating stuff isn't for the birds after all." He turned to Vlad. "Can we go through that again, Coach? With the music, I mean?"

Vlad glanced up at the clock. "It's already past six. I have an appointment with friends, but if you really want to . . ."

"Past six?" I blurted. "Oh, I'm sorry. I have to go."

"You can't stay five more minutes and go through it again?" Kai begged. "I just want to make sure it's all firm in my head."

"I can't," I apologized. "My school team is in

the play-offs. I have to be there for the start of the game, and Friday night traffic is murder."

"Are you a cheerleader or something?" Kai demanded.

"No. I told you my boyfriend's the quarterback. I promised I'd go to the game."

"He won't notice if you're five minutes late."

"Yes, he will. And I promised. I want to be there for him."

I saw Kai's questioning smirk, and I glared at him. "It's a play-off game. I have to be there."

"I've never seen him here watching you skate," Kai observed.

"He'd be here if it was important. If I asked him to come." I skated toward the edge of the rink. "And right now it's important that I'm there for him. So I have to run. See you guys. We'll work on the routine again in the morning. Okay?"

"Okay," Kai said flatly.

I snatched up my things and ran for the locker room on the side of the rink.

I drove like crazy through the Friday rush-hour traffic and barely made it to the game in time. Thankfully Troy was still doing pregame warmups on the field. He didn't even look in my direction once.

I found myself thinking that I could have stayed behind and gone through the routine again after all. And the moment I started thinking about the rink, the memory of what had happened to Kai and me came flooding back. I could feel Kai's powerful arms around me again, the music pulsing through us both. It was like magic, like nothing I had ever felt before. Not even when I was kissing Troy.

"We won!" I screamed, jumping to my feet. Around me the crowd had gone wild, everyone fighting to get to the field at once. I watched as Troy was swept toward the locker room by a wave of supporters. There was no way I could get near him, so I fought my way through the crowd and waited patiently outside the guys' locker room.

"Won't your mom have a fit if the entire football team shows up at your house?" I heard a girl say.

Then I recognized Tanya Schmid's giggle. Everyone knew Tanya. She was the blondest, most popular cheerleader at Berkeley High.

"They're in Vegas for the weekend. I'm not that stupid," Tanya said to her friend.

"So anyone could sleep over if they want to," the first girl said. "Hey, did you see who showed up at the game tonight? Kirsten Hayes."

Suddenly I was very interested in their conversation. I fought to hear them over the noisy crowd.

"Yeah. Too bad for me," Tanya said. "I don't know what Troy sees in her. She's never around for him. They can't go out during the week because she has to be in bed really early. Poor thing needs tons of beauty sleep."

"He'll get tired of her soon enough," the first girl said. "You know he never stays with one girl for more than a couple of months."

"That's what I'm planning on," Tanya added smugly. "I get the feeling my turn is coming real soon."

The noise of the crowd was getting louder, but I had heard enough. "Just let her try," I muttered to myself, my cheeks burning an angry red and my heart pounding in my chest.

It seemed like an eternity before Troy and his buddies came out of the locker room.

"Who's going to stop off to pick up the pizza and beer?" one of the guys yelled as they headed for the parking lot.

I saw Troy shove him. "Are you crazy? Keep your voice down. There are still teachers around." He lowered his voice. "Danny's doing it. He's got his brother's ID."

"See you at Tanya's house then," the first guy said.

I took a deep breath and stepped out of the shadows. "Hi."

Troy seemed surprised to see me. Was he expecting someone else? Maybe a certain very popular, very blond cheerleader?

He collected himself and smiled at me. "Oh, hi, Kirsten. Great game, huh?"

"Terrific. You were amazing."

"Yeah, I wasn't too bad. I didn't see you. It was so dark." Troy seemed uneasy as he gazed everywhere but at me.

You didn't even look for me, I almost said, but I didn't. There was no reason to start a fight. Not yet anyway.

"So, I guess you're going to the party at Tanya's house, right?" I asked innocently.

"Yeah, Tanya's house. That's right." Was it my imagination, or did he look suddenly uncomfortable?

"I don't know if I can stay out too late," I explained. "I have early morning practice."

"I thought you were off until noon on Saturdays."

"That was the old rink. This rink I skate early. Public skate is at two."

"You can come to the party for a little while, can't you?"

Part of me wanted to go, to make sure Tanya stayed away from Troy, but another part of me was upset that he'd ignored me, after making such a big deal about being there for him. Maybe if I said I was going home, Troy would realize I was upset. But then maybe he'd choose to be alone with Tanya. What if he didn't need me anymore?

"I can come for a while," I said. "Maybe I'll take my own car, in case I want to leave early."

I'd hoped he'd say that he'd drive me home whenever I wanted to leave, but he didn't. "Yeah, that might be a good idea."

By the time I pulled up in front of Tanya's house, the music was blasting from her front door. This definitely wasn't my sort of party, but I wasn't going to give Tanya the chance to be alone with Troy, not without a fight.

I looked in my rearview mirror and quickly brushed my hair. I wished I'd had more time to get ready before the game. I hadn't come prepared for a party.

Troy and the guys arrived just as I did, and everyone fell into a pizza-eating frenzy. I was about to join in when I thought about Kai. I couldn't afford to put on an ounce right now, or he'd tease me about weight lifting again. I grinned at the thought of his dimpled smile. He was kind of funny sometimes. Annoying but definitely funny.

I was just standing there, watching the crowd, when Joanne, a girl I knew from school, came over to join me. "How's the skating going, Kirsten?" she asked.

"Pretty good, thanks." I had to yell to be heard over the growing crowd.

"Still having trouble with that guy, or have you gotten him tamed yet?" she teased.

Joanne had eaten lunch with me a couple of days ago, and I had spent the entire hour complaining about Kai.

Troy turned around, a slice of pizza in his hand. "What guy? The Russian coach? Is he giving you trouble?"

"Not the coach, dummy," Joanne explained before I could answer. "Her new partner. The hockey hunk."

"Oh, him." Troy pretended he knew what she was talking about. He glared at me hard. Then

Joanne moved away, and Troy pounced on me. "New partner? You're skating with a partner now?"

"Well, uh . . . yeah."

"Why didn't you tell me?" Troy put the pizza down on an empty chair. Then he moved closer to me. So close, I could hardly breathe.

"It just happened, Troy," I said awkwardly. *Here goes,* I thought. "This is a trial period . . . to see if pairs skating is right for me. I didn't want to upset you. I was waiting until I was sure."

"And everyone else knows about it but me?" He moved closer.

"We haven't exactly had any time alone, have we?" I took a step back. Between Troy and the growing crowd, I was beginning to feel claustrophobic.

"You could have told me about it over the phone. Don't tell me it slipped your mind."

"It's no big deal, Troy. Coach wanted me to skate partners with this loser at the rink. Kai's not the easiest person to get along with. He has an ego the size of Texas and he's totally annoying."

"So why skate with him?"

I felt trapped. The room was getting hotter and hotter, and the noise level was unbearable.

"Because . . ." I stopped again, the powerful memory of the afternoon flooding back into my head. *Because something wonderful happens when we skate together.*

98

NINE

KAI AND I positioned ourselves at opposite ends of the rink from each other. It was early Saturday morning, and we were about to run through our freestyle program to music.

As the opening strains of the music began I counted the first four beats. Then with strong, solid strokes I skated backward across the rink toward Kai and prepared for a star lift. Kai's left hand closed tightly on mine, his right hand on my waist. With a powerful spring I jumped into his strong arms, then was suddenly high above his head.

"Here goes . . . ," Kai said. "Let's see if all that work in the gym paid off."

I held my breath as Kai let go of my left hand and held me by the waist. As he held me, suspended in the air with one hand, I felt as if I were flying. What an amazing feeling!

Effortlessly Kai placed me back onto the ice,

then we skated into a fun combination of dance steps. It was so natural . . . so perfect. And I couldn't keep myself from breaking out into a huge smile.

Next was the press lift. Kai and I had nailed this lift hundreds of times, so I went into the preparation confidently. Besides, we were in total sync . . . truly skating as one. I jumped, feeling strong. But just as Kai brought me down for the landing, I thought I spotted a familiar dark head in a football jacket leaning against the rink. Troy.

I completely lost all concentration and crashed hard on my butt.

"Ouch!" I moaned. Then I quickly stood up and skated toward Kai. I pretended I hadn't seen Troy. And I hoped Kai hadn't either. But as usual, I could never catch a break when it came to Kai.

"Hey, who's the dark-haired guy hanging out on the side of the rink? Do you know him?" Kai whispered to me as we went back to our routine. "He seems to know you. He can't stop staring at you."

I looked over to the barrier, pretending to have just noticed. "Oh, my gosh," I said. "It's Troy."

"Your boyfriend?"

Kai and I kept skating together. And suddenly I was very conscious of Kai's hands on my waist, his body close to mine. Every move now seemed suggestive. I tried to ignore Troy and continue skating, but I felt myself tensing up, wanting to hold Kai away from me. It was nearly impossible not to look over at Troy.

"What's he doing here?" I muttered.

"Did you give him a little talk about coming to cheer for you?"

"No, I didn't. In fact, I told him not to come until we'd had a chance to improve."

Kai grinned. "Maybe he doesn't trust you with me."

"That's definitely it," I said, picking up speed with two backward crossovers. "He was upset last night when I told him about you."

"He only found out last night? Why didn't you tell him before?"

"Big mistake, right? I don't know why I didn't tell him right away."

"Because I'm so gorgeous, you thought he'd be wildly jealous?" Kai teased as he grabbed my frozen right hand in his warm left one. I still hadn't gotten used to skating without my gloves.

"I told him he had nothing to worry about."

"He doesn't look too happy now." Kai spun me around.

"I wish I'd said you were one of those wimpy skating guys."

Kai's grin broadened. "The first compliment from you," he said sarcastically. "Not bad."

"Don't let it go to your head. I also told him you were a superbrat."

Now he really laughed. "Superbrat. I like that. Yeah. Good description." He gently slid his arms around my waist. "Let's go into that spin sequence where I hold you very close and run my

101

hands down your back. That'll really give him something to worry about."

"Behave yourself," I threatened.

"Well, he deserves it," Kai said. "What kind of a guy would come check up on his girlfriend just because she's skating with a partner?"

"I suppose I can understand it," I said as we skated a lively waltz step.

"Do you check up on him every time his football team has an away game? You know they ride the bus with the cheerleaders, don't you?"

"No, I don't check up on him," I said. *But maybe I should,* I thought. Kai was upsetting me. I'd never worried about those away games before, but last night had opened my eyes. I hadn't realized the cheerleaders spent so much time with the team. That Tanya Schmid spent so much time with Troy. I'd assumed they were like the marching band. You know . . . they practiced on their own and just showed up for the games. I guess skating so much had kept me a little in the dark about some things.

I could feel Troy's eyes staring at my back.

"I can't keep skating with him watching like this," I said, coming to an abrupt stop. "Can we take a break?"

"Kirsten? What's wrong?" Vlad called. "I thought the routine was coming along so well and now you stop in the middle?"

"I just need a minute, Coach. I have a guest I'd like to say hi to."

I put on my brightest smile as I skated over to Troy. "Hi! What a surprise! What are you doing here?" I asked as cheerfully as I could. Last night had been tense enough. Maybe if I pretended everything was okay, I thought, Troy would leave after a quick kiss and a hello.

"Oh, I wanted to check out a car-detailing place over in South City, so I thought I'd stop by and see how you were getting along."

Yeah, right, I thought. *What a coincidence!*

"So . . . you got home safely from the party last night?" he asked. He ran a hand through his dark brown hair. It was a little damp, probably from his shower. I had to admit, he sure looked good in his Berkeley High football jacket.

"Yeah, fine. Did you?" I countered, my eyes challenging him.

"Oh, sure. The party didn't last long after you left. The neighbors called and complained about the noise, so the cops broke it up."

"What a pity," I said.

I waited for Troy to say more. But he just looked around, his eyes focusing on Kai, who was talking to Vlad in the middle of the rink.

"You . . . uh, looked pretty impressive out there," Troy finally said. "Very athletic."

"Yeah, well, pairs skating is very gymnastic," I explained. "You should see all the work we do in the gym to get those lifts right." I tried a carefree laugh. "Kai says that lifting me is worse than lifting weights in the gym. He's so rude to me."

Why was this conversation so awkward? I wondered. This was Troy—my boyfriend. I'd never had a problem talking to him before, but everything was different now. Something was going on. Was it because of Tanya?

At that moment Kai skated over to the barrier, coming to an impressive hockey stop beside us. "Hey, Kirsten, don't stop now. We were just getting into a groove together. We don't want to break that magic, do we?"

I glared at him, my eyes warning him to behave or else. "I'll be right back," I said to Kai. "I'm just saying hello to my boyfriend. He came to watch us practice. Isn't that sweet of him?" I turned back to Troy. "Troy drove over all the way from Berkeley."

"Your boyfriend?" Kai demanded. "You didn't tell me you had a boyfriend." He honestly sounded hurt. I could have killed him. I knew that Kai was teasing me, but I didn't think Troy was finding it very funny.

Troy cleared his throat.

"Kai's just joking. I'm always talking about you, Troy," I reassured him.

"Yeah, right," Troy said, shifting his gaze from me to Kai and back again.

"Troy, this is my skating partner, Kai. Kai, this is my boyfriend, Troy."

Kai held out his hand. "Hi, Troy, glad to meet you. I expect our Kirsten's told you all about me."

"Oh, uh . . . yes," Troy lied. "And she wasn't

too complimentary. She told me you were a major pain in the butt."

Kai laughed and ruffled my hair. "She's such a little kidder. Actually Kirsten and I kid around a lot—know what I mean?" He winked at Troy. "But when we're on the ice together and the music is playing . . . it's magic." He pretended to fan himself with his hand. "I mean, bring on the air-conditioning, it gets so hot in here. Right, Kirsten?" He laughed and thumped Troy on the shoulder. "No offense, guy, but I can understand why she's kept quiet about us. We didn't mean it to happen; it just did. Talk about chemistry. We've tried to ignore it, but I suppose we're just acting out our true feelings on the ice."

"What are you talking about?" I demanded, turning to face Kai.

"You and me. This relationship we've got."

"Relationship? What relationship?" I said angrily. "Don't listen to a word he says, Troy. Kai's just mouthing off. It's all lies. We don't have a relationship. We don't even *like* each other."

"It sure didn't look that way when you were skating out there," Troy said. "This guy's hands were all over you."

"It's just part of the routine. That's how pairs skating routines are."

"If that's true, then I don't want to watch anymore," Troy said bitterly. "I certainly don't want to feel like a fool while this loser has his hands on you. And maybe I don't need a

105

girlfriend who lets another guy touch her like that."

"Maybe the guy she's with isn't paying her enough attention," Kai cut in. "Maybe he just isn't exciting enough for her."

"You want to step outside and settle this right now?" Troy threatened, leaning over the barrier.

"Sure. Anytime. But I should warn you that I used to be a hockey player. No holds barred." Kai pretended to fight the air.

"C'mon, guys." I laughed nervously, stepping between them. "You're acting like children. Cut it out."

I'd never imagined that I'd have two guys fighting over me. I guess I should have been flattered and excited, but I wasn't. I was scared.

I put my hand on Troy's arm. "Calm down, Troy. He's only doing this to annoy you. Believe me, there's no truth to anything Kai says. If you'd shown up at any other time, you'd have found us fighting. That's what we do ninety-nine percent of the time. Kai just gets a kick out of stirring up trouble." I turned to glare at Kai, who looked as if he might burst out laughing any second.

"We'll talk later—when this *loser* isn't around," Troy said menacingly.

"I'm not the one who's acting like a loser right now," Kai said smoothly. "Kirsten and I want to get back to work. You're wasting our time here, buddy."

"Maybe you should go, Troy," I said, looking up at him, begging him to understand. "We really can't practice with you watching. You have nothing to worry about. Honest. I have no interest in Kai. He's my skating partner and he bugs the heck out of me, just like he's doing now."

Troy stalked off. "Remember what I said, Kirsten!" he yelled over his shoulder. "And tell that guy to watch where he puts his hands!" He stormed out, the swing doors clattering shut behind him.

As soon as I could swallow the tears gathering in my throat, I marched up to Kai, my cold fists balled at my sides.

"Why did you do that?" I accused. My voice trembled with anger. "You're the world's biggest jerk. I know you think you're funny, but you're not. I almost lost my boyfriend and it's all your fault."

"Why did I do what?" Kai demanded. "What's all my fault?"

"Why did you just lie to Troy . . . make him believe there's something going on between us?"

"Get real. You deserve someone better than that muscle head."

"Oh, so you made your decision based on this one meeting? Are you a world-famous expert on relationships?"

He wasn't smiling now. He was looking at me seriously. "I've watched the way you rush off every night so you don't miss his calls. I saw how keyed up you were yesterday because you were afraid you'd miss part of his dumb football game. That guy doesn't want a girlfriend—he wants another fan." Kai glided across the ice.

"It's really none of your business, Kai. Besides, Troy is sweet to me. He could have any girl he wants at school . . . and he wants me."

"Is that why you stay with him? Because he's a trophy guy?"

"Of course not," I said quickly, skating to catch up to him. "I love him."

"I don't think you do," Kai said. "I think he boosts your ego."

"That's not true," I snapped, and stopped moving.

"You should go out with a guy because you have fun together, and quite frankly, that guy doesn't look like much fun to me."

"As if you'd have a good time seeing your girl-friend with another guy."

"If I made a commitment to a girl, I'd trust her completely." He shook his head. "I can't help it if you're afraid to tell Troy the truth. It's not my fault he's so jealous and possessive. What's your problem, Kirsten?"

"You, Kai!" I screamed. "You've been my problem since the first time we met."

TEN

"KIRSTEN, YOU'RE HAVING a bad day today. You are not concentrating," Vlad commented after I had stumbled on a change of edges.

After my blowup with Troy and Kai, I could barely concentrate on breathing, let alone skating. I was too upset to focus.

"No kidding," I said, pushing a stray hair back into my ponytail.

"Is something bothering you? Your visitor, perhaps?" Vlad asked.

I nodded. "It's all Kai's fault. Kai and his stupid teasing. He told Troy that we're attracted to each other. That we're more than just skating partners. I said it wasn't true, but I don't think Troy believed me."

"This is why I don't want visitors at my practice sessions." Vlad looked steamed as he threw up his hands. "It always upsets my skaters. Look at

Alice. She goes to pieces when her mother shows up." He patted me on the shoulder. "Kai is a foolish boy. But that's no reason to stop skating. Now get back to work." He frowned at Kai.

Kai looked at Vlad defiantly. "It wasn't foolish. The guy's a loser. Look at how he treats Kirsten. He doesn't deserve her."

"That's really none of your business, Kai. Maybe I like Troy just the way he is," I countered.

Kai looked at me solemnly. "Then you're not as smart as I thought you were."

"Butt out of my life!" I yelled as I skated across the ice and stood, gripping the cold wood of the railing in my hands. For once I was burning up. I needed to cool off.

"What was that all about?" Alice asked later when we were sitting in the locker room. It was before two on Saturday afternoon, and practice had just ended.

"Kai really bugs me," I snapped as I unlaced my right boot. "Did you see the way he acted when Troy was here? Trying to pretend that we were more than just skating partners—what nerve! He's the last guy I'd ever date. I don't think I even want to skate with him anymore."

"You know, pairs partners have been known to fall in love," Alice teased. "Look at Ekaterina Gordeeva and Sergei Grinkov. They were partners for years before they fell in love and were married."

I nodded. Gordeeva and her late husband were my inspiration.

"Just think, if you marry Kai, you'll be known as the mighty Bergstroms," Alice said.

Love. Kai? I had never used those two words in the same sentence before. I did love skating with Kai, but he definitely wasn't boyfriend material. Right now he was barely *human* material. I couldn't help but wonder, though, what it would be like to date Kai. Would we have anything but insults to say to each other?

I pulled off my right skate and listened to what Alice was saying.

"Well, watching you two together . . . it looks so incredible when you're in his arms." Alice leaned closer to me. "It wouldn't surprise me if you guys got together one day. What's it like when he holds you close to him?"

I wanted to tell her that something incredible happened when the music started. That I forgot about the annoying side of Kai when we were on the ice. We just seemed to melt together, skate as one. But I was suddenly shy about saying it out loud.

I grinned. "Most of the time I'm terrified he's going to drop me. It's really hard to keep your balance out there when you're moving so fast."

"Yeah, I guess it must be."

"Especially with someone like Kai. You never know when he's going to pull some dumb trick on you," I added.

"But you guys do look great together. I almost

wish I couldn't do the triple and you could. Then I could be skating with Kai instead of you."

"But you're doing so well on your own. Your jumps look great, Alice."

She bit her heart-shaped lip. "I just hope I don't blow it at Sectionals. I'm a nervous wreck when I have to compete."

"You'll be fine," I reassured her. "When you hear the music and you skate out onto the ice, you'll forget that anybody is watching you. I always do."

"You do?" She looked at me suspiciously. "You're so lucky. I always see my mother's face, right there by the barrier." She sighed. "She wants to send me to a sports psychiatrist to build my confidence."

"That might help you," I said, looking at her big, dark eyes.

She shook her head. "I don't need a psychiatrist. My mom does!"

Poor Alice, I thought as I came out of the rink. She was a terrific skater, but it must have been horrible to be so nervous all the time. At least I loved performing. I loved skating in front of an audience, feeling the electricity flowing between me and the crowd. I couldn't wait for the big time, for the Olympics and TV. And I got the feeling that Kai couldn't either, regardless of what he said.

I bet he'll ham it up in front of the cameras, I thought. I smiled at the thought of him on the ice . . .

until I remembered how furious I was at him.

I hoped he hadn't completely blown my chance to be with Troy. I'd just call Troy, explain that Kai was a stuck-up troublemaker, that he was the last person on earth I'd ever get involved with off the ice. That would smooth things out.

But as I drove home, I couldn't stop thinking about everything Kai had said about Troy. What did he know about Troy and me anyway? I was more than just a fan to Troy. And he was more than just a "trophy guy" to me. We had fun whenever we were together, didn't we?

I thought about all the great times I'd had with Troy—the parties and movies and pizza after football games—and I realized one thing. We always did what *Troy* wanted to do. We never once hung out with *my* friends, went out to a restaurant where *I* wanted to eat. Sure, Troy was sweet and caring, but he liked to get his own way. He wanted to be number one in our relationship.

Was Kai right after all? I knew I was still dazzled by Troy. I was still flattered every time we went out. Maybe it was time I started believing that I was special too.

As soon as I got home, I rushed to the phone and called Troy. But no one answered. I hoped this wouldn't be a repeat of the last time we'd had a misunderstanding . . . when I'd left him on hold that night on the phone. I didn't know where Troy could be. But I did know one thing: Troy was upset. And I was pretty sure he'd intentionally stayed away from home. He knew when I got home on Saturdays. And I usually called and made plans for that night.

I called him later that day, but again . . . no answer. On Sunday morning I tried him, but this time his mother said he'd gone fishing with his father. By Sunday night it was my turn to be mad. I decided to test him. I forced myself not to call again. I'd wait and see how long it would take Troy to call me himself. But he never called.

I didn't see Troy again until Monday at school when he passed me in the hall with a casual, "Hi, Kirsten."

I ran to catch up with him. "Why didn't you call me this weekend? Are you mad at me?"

"Mad? Why would I be mad?"

"You know, all those dumb things Kai said at the rink on Saturday."

Troy shrugged. "If you want to choose a loser like that over me, then that's your problem."

"That's the point, Troy. I told you Kai's just my skating partner." I was standing directly in front of him. The halls were crowded, so we moved close to the wall to avoid being bumped in the rush of students. "We work together and fight a lot, that's all. Believe me, if I was looking for another boyfriend, it wouldn't be him. Don't you know I'd never go behind your back? You can trust me, Troy."

"You went behind your coach's back once. Remember Myra," he said slowly.

"For you!" I snapped. "I did it for you." But I

114

sensed his reasoning. If I could lie and cheat once, then maybe I could do it again. "Fine," I said angrily. "If you don't want to believe me, don't."

He grabbed my arm as I turned to walk away. "It's okay, Kirsten. I believe you. It was just kind of a shock, seeing you with that guy."

I took a deep breath. "It was kind of a shock to me too, when I found out that you'd planned to go to Tanya's party Friday night with or without me."

"What are you talking about?" he demanded, looking around uneasily.

"You never mentioned her party to me."

"I just assumed we'd go together."

"Tanya didn't," I said quietly.

"What are you talking about?" Troy seemed suddenly nervous and uncomfortable.

"Tanya wanted to get you alone at that party. She's got a major crush on you, which I'm sure you already know. Come to think of it, how was the party after I left? Did anything happen that I should know about?"

"Oh, come on, Kirsten. You don't think I'd cheat on you with Tanya, do you?"

"Well, maybe that's why you thought I'd been cheating with Kai." I looked him straight in the eye now. "Maybe your guilty conscience made you believe it could be true."

We stood there, staring at each other, while the herds of students streamed around us. Everyone was hurrying off to class. The final bell rang.

"This is stupid," Troy said, adjusting his

books from his right hand to his left. "I can't talk about this here. I've got to get to class."

What was wrong with us? I just came to apologize to Troy . . . make him understand that I wanted to be with him, not Kai. But all we did was fight. My relationship with Troy was becoming as difficult as my relationship with Kai.

"If I enter a team in a competition, it has to be a team worthy of me," Vlad told us Monday afternoon. Vlad had become merciless. In addition to an hour a day in the gym and four hours on the ice, Vlad pushed us to learn new spins and lifts every day. "My reputation is on the line. If you skate poorly, then everyone will say, 'Poor old Vladimir, he's not as good as he used to be. He's gone soft since he came to America.'" He looked from Kai's face to mine. "That's why you must not let me down."

That week we were learning the death spiral. It was about as scary as it sounded. The death spiral was a difficult move, one that meant I had to trust Kai completely. Kai was supposed to spin me around, holding me by the hand. I had to keep my body in a straight line, sliding my feet out farther and farther from him until I was almost horizontal to the ice. And in a perfect death spiral my head was only supposed to be an inch or two from the surface of the ice.

It took major concentration to keep myself from getting scared or arching my back as I sensed my head nearing the ice. I couldn't stop bizarre visions of how my brain would look, splattered all over the glossy surface. I tried to relax, but I couldn't. I pulled up every time at the very last second.

"It is perfectly safe, Kirsten. Kai won't let go of you!" Vlad yelled. "You have to trust your partner, Kirsten."

Yeah, right, I thought. *How am I supposed to trust Kai when he's the reason my life is falling apart?*

By Friday we still hadn't gotten the hang of it.

"Come on, we have to get this," Kai encouraged. "We can do it, Kirsten. It's not that hard."

"Not for you, it's not," I said, rubbing my hands against my gray wool tights to warm them. "You try being the one whose head hits the ice."

"I won't let your head hit the ice, Kirsten. I promise. You have to trust me if we're going to skate together."

"Yeah, you've given me every reason to trust you, haven't you? You lie to my boyfriend and practically break us up. You laugh when I fall and hurt myself. Give me one good reason why I should trust you."

"Because I made you a promise," he said quietly. "You might not believe this, but I'm not a violent person. I don't want to hurt you."

This new, sincere Kai was difficult to take. Any second I expected him to yell, "Psych!" or "Not!" and burst out laughing. But he didn't.

"Enough for today," Vlad interrupted us around six that night. "You have both worked hard all week. I must leave on time tonight for a dinner date."

"Ooh, Vlad's got a date," Kai teased.

"With several old Russian gentlemen at a Russian restaurant in San Francisco, in case you get any strange ideas," Vlad said as he headed for the side of the rink. Alice and the other skaters, who had been working on their own, followed him. Kai and I were left alone.

"See you tomorrow then," I said to Kai as I headed off the ice.

Kai grabbed my arm. "Do you want to stay on and work on that death spiral a little longer? I'd really like to nail it before we leave tonight. I think we're so close." He paused and looked at me. "Or do you have to rush off to one of Troy's football games?"

"No, I don't have to rush off. Troy doesn't have a game tonight. Besides . . . I'm not just one of his 'fans.' I can do whatever I want."

"Great," Kai said. "Will you stay then?"

"Do you think we should work on it without Vlad around?" I asked, pulling a tissue from the left sleeve of my brown sweater. Vlad had just disappeared through the swing doors.

"Wouldn't it be neat to surprise Vlad with a perfect death spiral in the morning?" Kai asked. "Maybe it'll be easier with the ice to ourselves. We won't have to worry about bumping into anybody. The Zamboni won't come out for another fifteen minutes. C'mon, Kirsten, let's give it a shot."

"Okay." My voice echoed around the empty rink. I was suddenly very conscious that I was completely alone with Kai. I looked around nervously.

"Great, let's get to work," Kai said, holding his hand out to me.

We started the death spiral again. I tried to focus on trusting Kai and letting go, but it wasn't easy. I hated the fact that my fate completely rested in Kai's strong hands. The tension pulled at my entire body.

In the distance we heard an outer door slam as the last person left the rink. Around us was total silence. You could hear the hiss of our skate blades against the ice and even the sharp intake of our breath. The maintenance men were probably in their office, waiting to bring the Zamboni out onto the ice. It felt as if we were the only two people in the world.

"Let's skate through the routine, up to the point where we do the death spiral," Kai suggested as he took off his bulky gray sweater to reveal a tight black turtleneck underneath. I couldn't help but notice the material pulling at his muscular chest. "Maybe it will be easier if we lead into it like that."

We started skating together. There was no music, so we counted as we moved across the ice. One. Two. Three. Four . . . and the magical feeling returned. We did our side-by-side flying camels and came together for the combination spin. Then Kai took my hand and I went flying out into the death spiral.

119

We'd never taken it so fast before. I felt the cold rising up from the surface of the ice as I dropped lower and lower and lower. The lights flashed in a blur above my head. Closing my eyes, I felt myself stretch into a perfect, elegant line, like a pencil being drawn over the surface of the ice.

It seemed like an eternity before Kai pulled me back up to my feet beside him.

"Yes! We did it, Kirsten!" he cheered, his voice echoing off the empty stadium seats around us. "You were incredible. We're going to blow them away at that competition! We're going to the Nationals. Correction—we're going all the way to the Olympics!"

He swept me into his arms and spun around with me. Kai's face was alive and happy, as I'd never seen it before. I was laughing crazily too, caught up in the excitement of the moment. Then he lowered me to my feet, his arms still tightly around me. My arms were wrapped around his neck, and his eyes looked straight into mine. Suddenly we weren't laughing anymore.

Slowly, as if drawn by an invisible magnet, our mouths came together. I wasn't prepared for the incredible electric current that raced through my body at his touch. My heart was pounding. I was floating, light as a feather. As I closed my eyes, I could feel Kai's heart hammering against mine. And I never wanted that moment to end. . . .

ELEVEN

IDON'T KNOW how long Kai and I stood in the middle of the rink, locked in each other's arms, before we suddenly broke apart. Kai's red face looked as embarrassed as mine felt.

"I guess we both, uh . . . got a little carried away," he stammered. Then he laughed. "I don't think we should put that kiss into the routine, though. We don't want to get an NC-17 rating."

A million thoughts raced through my mind. I'd just kissed Kai, a guy I didn't even like, and I wanted to do it again. I'd never felt so carried away from a kiss before, not even when I kissed Troy, and it scared me.

"Oh, no. Look at the time." I glanced at the large clock on the wall, acting as if I were really surprised. "I should get going. The traffic is always terrible on Fridays. I don't want my parents to worry, and Troy will probably call. We usually do stuff on Fridays and . . . Kai, I, uh . . . really have to go." I could hear myself babbling.

He took my hand. "Don't worry about it, Kirsten," he soothed. "We got swept up in the heat of the moment. We were both excited, that's all. It's no big deal. Don't get upset about it."

"Upset? Who says I'm upset?" I tried to give him my brightest smile. "At least we nailed the death spiral. I guess that's worth a little kiss."

"Sure," he said. "It was definitely worth it."

"I really do have to go," I said, although my feet didn't seem to want to move.

"Yeah, I guess we should clear out of here, let the guy who drives the Zamboni finish up before evening public skate," Kai said. "And I have stuff to do." He gave an embarrassed laugh. Then he said, "See ya, Kirstie."

"See you, Kai."

I usually hated it when people called me Kirstie, but from Kai it sounded just right.

I watched Kai skate ahead of me to the edge of the ice. Usually he came to a graceful halt, smoothly gliding off the ice. But today he tripped over his skates, as if his legs had a mind of their own. I knew how he felt. My legs felt like jelly too as I slowly made my way to the locker room.

My icy fingers trembled as I unlaced my boots. I was really confused. I mean, really, *really* confused. Was it just, as Kai had said, the heat of the moment that had made him kiss me that way? Correction, made *us* kiss that way. Maybe it was natural to kiss someone after you'd just completed a difficult move. But that didn't explain the way he'd made me feel. I felt as if I were soaring, flying outside of my body. It felt as if I'd kissed the guy of my dreams.

Had he felt the same way? Kai seemed to be as shaken up as I was. He'd never tripped over his skates before. But he'd joked about it afterward, said it wasn't a big deal. Maybe it didn't mean anything to him. And if I was smart, it wouldn't affect me either.

Besides, it was dangerous to get romantically involved with your partner. Especially a partner like Kai. He was so wild and totally unpredictable. I mean, what would happen if we broke up? How could we continue to skate together? It would be way too complicated.

And then there was Troy. I couldn't throw everything away with Troy because of one harmless, little—fantastic—kiss.

"We have to talk." Kai's voice behind me made me jump.

It was early Saturday morning, and the dimly lit rink was filled with the muffled sound of blades cutting into the fresh ice. Alice and the other skaters wove their way among the shadows, warming up before practice.

I was slowly circling the rink, begging my legs to wake up. The rest of me wasn't very awake either. I held back a yawn. I hadn't gotten much sleep the night before. I'd tossed and turned, dreaming of Kai's magical kiss.

"Let's be grown up about this," Kai continued. "I don't think you want to risk everything we've worked so hard at over one silly kiss."

In the shadowy light I noticed that Kai couldn't look me in the eye. I was having a hard time looking at him myself.

I rubbed my chilled hands along my legs and skated in a circle in front of Kai.

"Do you think you can work with me as if nothing happened last night?" he asked.

"I don't see why not. We'll just pretend that yesterday never happened . . . except for the death spiral. I still can't believe we nailed it. Let's get to work." And with that I skated backward away from Kai.

The rest of Saturday's practice was a mess. Kai and I were extrapolite to each other, as if we were embarrassed to touch each other. I didn't quite know how to act around him anymore.

Vlad definitely noticed something was wrong. "No, Kirsten, that was terrible!" Vlad yelled after I'd messed up a simple jump. "Stop holding back. Relax, feel the ice beneath your skates. Enjoy each other."

I nodded, determined to shake my awkwardness. I skated toward Kai, my hand meeting his. Kai's hand was unusually sweaty when I attempted to jump. And his arm wasn't strong and secure. Then halfway through the lift I fell for the hundredth time that day.

"Okay, you two. That's enough for today. I can't take another minute of such horrible skating. I will not tolerate such sloppy work from either of you again."

For once Kai seemed to be at a loss for words. He just stared down at his skates.

"Sorry, Coach," I blurted, unable to look at Vlad. "It won't happen again."

When practice ended, I tried to slip out quickly, hoping to avoid everyone. But it wasn't my lucky day.

Alice grabbed me as I made my way to the women's locker room. "Okay. Tell me everything," she demanded. "What's going on with you and Kai? You guys have been acting strange all day."

"It's so weird, Alice," I began. "Last night we nailed the death spiral. It was perfect. And then suddenly we were in each other's arms, kissing. Right in the middle of the ice."

"Kai kissed you? I c-can't believe it," Alice stammered as she pulled a brand-new pair of silver exercise pants over her gorgeous blue unitard. "I always thought . . . I mean—you two fight all the time."

"I know. It's crazy. I can't believe it either." I finished untying my laces.

"What happened afterward?"

I shrugged. "Kai just laughed it off, said it was no big deal."

"What was the kiss like?" she asked, leaning close to me. It was as if she were afraid she'd miss some juicy detail if she didn't pay close attention.

"Amazing, breathtaking. I never knew a kiss could be so great," I blurted. I kicked off my skate and sent it flying across the rubber matting. "But that's not the point. I don't know what to do, Alice. I keep telling myself it was nothing, just an innocent kiss, but I'm not sure I believe it. I mean, I'm still into Troy, I think. Even though we haven't really been getting along very well recently. Oh, how can I be in love with one guy and feel so totally incredible when I kiss another?"

"Maybe Kai's just a good kisser," Alice suggested. "He's probably had lots of practice."

"Yeah," I said uncertainly. After all, I didn't know anything about Kai, about his personal life. Maybe he was the kind of guy who kissed girls all the time. Maybe it really hadn't meant anything to him. And suddenly I realized how odd it was that I didn't know about Kai's personal life. About why he couldn't go back to hockey . . . about what he liked and didn't like. We'd spent so much time together, but we'd never actually had a real conversation.

"I'd forget about it if I were you," Alice said. "You've got a great boyfriend. Why would you want to ruin a perfectly fun relationship for a guy like Kai?"

"I just wish it had never happened. Life would be so much less complicated. It feels so strange every time Kai holds me now. I don't know what to think anymore."

"Don't worry so much, Kirsten. By tomorrow

Kai will probably make this whole thing into a joke."

"You're right. I'm making way too much out of it. I'm going to have to find a way to forget all about Kai."

I decided to surprise Troy by showing up at the play-off game over in San Ramon that afternoon. Our team played great, and I couldn't help but notice how confident Troy was. He kept his cool even when the other team rushed at him from all sides. He nailed the ball directly into our receiver's hands time after time. I wanted to nudge the fans next to me and say, "That's my boyfriend out there." Even if we hadn't been getting along.

But I couldn't completely shake Kai from my mind. If our partnership worked out, Kai and I would be together day after day for many years to come. I didn't know whether to be excited or terrified at that thought.

"Good game, huh?" Troy interrupted my thoughts as he found me after the game. He seemed more than surprised to see me. He almost seemed upset as he leaned down and gave me a sweaty kiss.

Nope . . . nothing. No magic when Troy kissed me anymore. I suddenly wondered if there ever had been. . . .

"You were wonderful," I said, taking in his messy brown hair and dirty uniform. "You get better every week, Troy."

He draped a sweaty arm around my shoulders.

"Look, Kirsten, I didn't know you were coming to the game today. I made plans with the guys. Besides, don't you need to spend more time with your partner?"

"What's that supposed to mean, Troy?" I pulled out of his shoulder and forced myself to look him in the eye.

"C'mon, Kirsten. Everyone knows you're too busy with your hockey hunk to hang out with me. I'm the laughingstock of the team. And I just don't know how much more I can deal with." Troy's voice cracked slightly as he shifted his helmet from his left side to his right.

"It's not like that, Troy, and you know it. Kai's just my partner, that's all. I thought you were okay with this." Now my voice was shaking.

"Well, I'm not," Troy snapped, and turned on his heel.

"Troy . . . ," I called after him, but he was already swallowed up in the crowd.

I was upset about that scene with Troy, but not for the reasons you might think. I wasn't sad that our feelings seemed to be far from love for each other. I was angry that Troy had accused me of choosing Kai over him.

I spent the rest of the weekend thinking about Troy. About all the fun we'd had those first few weeks. About the fact that now our relationship had completely fallen apart. I had been so flattered, so excited by Troy's attention at first. He'd shown me how much fun a normal teenager could have—going to parties and football games and movies. But I wasn't a "normal" teenager. I was an ice skater. And if I planned to achieve my Olympic dreams, I knew what I had to do.

I hadn't been fair to Troy . . . to myself. I thought I could have it all . . . a great boyfriend—a social life—and still have plenty of time for practice. But now I knew that was impossible.

Monday morning I planned to talk to Troy . . . tell him that I liked him, but that we both needed different things. Troy needed someone to adore him, someone who could drop everything at a moment's notice . . . someone to cheer her lungs out at every home and away game. Actually Troy didn't need a girlfriend . . . he needed a cheerleader. And I was sure one blond cheerleader who threw loud parties in particular would be very happy with my decision to break up with Troy.

I, on the other hand, needed more. And unless I could find a guy who could accept that skating came first with me, I planned to stay far away from that scene for a while. I needed a strong, sensitive guy. Someone who wasn't defined by his girlfriend. The next guy I fell for would have to be confident, be sure of himself, be able to stand alone. Because he'd be spending lots of nights and weekends without me.

I rehearsed my speech all through math class on Monday until it sounded pretty good to me. I planned to be honest with Troy . . . let him down easily. I was sure it wouldn't come as a shock.

After all, we were barely even speaking to each other at this point. But as I saw Troy slowly approach me in the crowded hallway, all my carefully rehearsed words flew out of my head.

"Hi, Kirsten . . ." Troy didn't sound happy to see me. He didn't look too great either. His usually bright brown eyes seemed tired and almost gray.

"Hi." *Here goes,* I thought. *It's now or never.* I took Troy's arm and pulled him toward a wall lined with lockers. "Troy—"

"Kirsten—" Troy and I spoke at the same time. He seemed unusually uncomfortable, almost nervous. Did he know what I was about to say? He hadn't once looked me in the eye, and he was fidgeting with the books in his hands, moving them from his right hand to his left, then back to his right again.

"You first," we both said again.

"Okay." I smiled, taking control of the conversation. "Well, Troy, I need to tell you something," I began.

"Good, 'cause I need to talk to you too, Kirsten," Troy interrupted. "It's pretty obvious that you don't have any time to be with me these days. . . . I guess you never did." He paused, looked around the crowded hall, then looked at me. "I like you, Kirsten. And I'm proud of what you're doing—"

"Thanks, Troy. That's kind of what I wanted to talk about—"

"But I can't go on like this anymore," he continued as if I hadn't even spoken. "I need a girlfriend who's there for me, Kirsten. Someone who wants to spend all her free time with me . . . not some other guy on the ice. I'm sick of getting grief from the guys on the team for always being alone. It's not right for the captain of the football team to be without his girlfriend after every practice and game."

I couldn't believe what I was hearing. *Troy* was breaking up with *me*.

"I know I sound selfish, but these are the play-offs. Soon we'll be playing all over the state," he explained, his right hand reaching out to touch my arm. It was as if he were actually trying to console me. He probably thought I'd break out into some tearful scene any minute now. Then he could play the sensitive guy . . . easing my pain with a simple touch of his hand.

The strange thing was, I didn't feel sad. I was angry. How dare Troy break up with me just because I was too busy to be his lovesick puppy?

"I need a girl who can support me, someone who thinks what I'm doing is important."

"I never said football wasn't important, Troy. I think you guys are great," I jumped in. I wasn't about to let him make me the bad guy now. "But . . ."

"But your skating is more important."

"To me, it is." I took a step away from him. "It has to be if I plan to make it all the way."

Troy looked around as if he were trying to find a way to end the painful conversation . . . a way to escape. "So you understand, don't you? You agree that we should break up. I mean, it's not as if we've been getting along recently. We haven't even been out together these past few weeks."

"Yeah, Troy. I understand. And I agree."

We stood there, barely looking at each other. It was as if we were afraid to walk away. Because that would mean that it was official. That we were no longer a couple.

The hallway had emptied out as the bell rang.

"I have to go," Troy finally said.

"Me too."

"See you around then, Kirsten." And with that we went our separate ways.

The rest of the day went by in a blur. I felt awkward and embarrassed and a little hurt. But most of all I was relieved. Now that Troy and I were through, I could focus all my energy on the competition that was less than a month away.

The last thing I wanted to do that afternoon was skate. I came out onto the ice to find Kai standing there all alone, seemingly lost in thought. I couldn't stop myself from noticing the way his light brown hair glowed in the fluorescent lights. The way his tight black turtleneck defined his strong shoulders and back. I felt my insides do a flip-flop.

This can't be happening, I told myself. *I can't be interested in Kai. I'm just feeling lonely and vulnerable after breaking up with Troy.*

But when Kai skated over to me with his hand outstretched, I couldn't help myself. I gave in to him. I took his hand and felt a rush of electricity jolt my insides again. Just like when we'd kissed.

We started skating together, slowly at first. It was a bit awkward, but things got easier after a while. I was surprised that we were able to have such a good practice session that day. I was sure thoughts of my breakup with Troy would interfere, break my focus. But I was wrong. Because once Kai touched me with his strong hand, Troy vanished from my every thought. Suddenly it was me and Kai against the world.

Vlad seemed surprised too. And he was really impressed with our death spiral. "You see what happens when you work well together?" Vlad asked.

I snuck a glance at Kai, who seemed to be beaming with pride as I was.

"Now we can go on and finish up the routine," Vlad said. "Then you get to try the whole thing with music again."

"Kirsten, I . . . uh, wanted to ask you something," Kai whispered as Vlad made his way to the center of the rink. He had left his notes in a pile on the ice.

Kai and I skated to the edge of the rink.

My heart started pounding. "Yes?"

"Do you really think we have a chance at Nationals?" Kai cleaned some ice off his right blade. "You know all about this figure-skating stuff. How do we match up?"

"You've seen the videos," I said, relieved. I was afraid he wanted to talk about Friday night again.

"Yeah, those videos Vlad showed us of the pairs from the last Olympics. I know we're not in their league yet. But do you think we'll qualify for Nationals?"

"I hope so," I said. "I think we have a good chance. We're getting there, aren't we?"

He looked thoughtful. "It's a scary thought. This time last year I didn't even know what pairs skating was. I planned on being a big-league hockey player. And now I've got this new future stretched out ahead of me—I'm not sure I'm ready for it."

Suddenly I heard a noise just off the ice. I looked up as a loud group of guys stormed in. I felt Kai stiffen beside me as the powerfully built guys pushed and shoved one another, acting as if they owned the place.

"Look, there he is. Hey, Kai, get over here!" I heard a guy in a San Jose Sharks jacket yell out.

"Oh, no," Kai muttered. He turned away from me and skated over to them. "What are you guys doing here?" I heard him ask.

I stood there watching Kai's back as he talked to them. It didn't take a genius to figure out that they were his hockey teammates. I tried to edge closer, hoping to hear what they were saying. I felt my heart race. Had they come to take Kai away from me—to persuade him to go back to hockey? Was I about to lose him forever?

I couldn't believe the incredible wave of despair that shot through me. I had to stop myself from skating over and dragging him away. I wanted to yell, "He's mine now. You can't have him back." But I stayed where I was, straining to hear what they were saying.

Kai turned and pointed me out. "That's my partner, Kirsten, over there," he said. "We're in the middle of practice."

They looked at me with amused smirks, as if they thought that Kai was kidding them. I got the feeling he didn't want me to meet them, so I stayed away—although I was dying to find out the truth about his hockey days.

Maybe one of those guys could tell me what had happened to Kai, why he wouldn't play anymore. But I couldn't do that to Kai. If he wanted me to know, he'd tell me himself.

"Why don't you come back to hockey, man?" I heard a deep voice ask. "This isn't for you! Forget about what happened. Nobody remembers it anymore."

"I do," Kai said. "I remember everything." He turned to skate to me. "I have to get back to work now, guys. But I'll be in touch. I'll think about it, okay?"

"Yeah, think about it, buddy," the biggest guy in the group said, slapping Kai on the shoulder.

"We miss you, Kai," another guy called out.

Kai skated toward me, a look of pain across his face. Something more than a simple injury must have happened on that hockey rink. Until now I'd believed he was here to keep fit, waiting for an injury to completely heal. Now it seemed more serious than that.

He took my hand and dragged me across the ice.

"What was that all about?" I asked.

"Those were my old teammates." He checked over his shoulder to make sure they had left. "They came here to talk me into playing again."

"And what did you say?"

"I'm here, aren't I?" he snapped.

"There's no need to bite my head off," I snapped back. "I just asked an innocent question. I mean, there's nothing wrong with you—you're strong and healthy. I'm sure you could go back to hockey anytime you wanted. That's why I can't help wondering—"

"Well, don't," he cut in. "You told me to butt out of your life, so do me a favor and keep out of mine."

I was furious and hurt. But at that moment I didn't care. I couldn't take any more emotional confrontations that day. First the breakup with Troy and now this. I had to get out of there. I needed to be alone.

I was halfway to the locker room—tears flowing down my face—when Kai grabbed me. "Kirsten, wait up," he called.

"Let go of me. I've had it. Go back to your hockey friends and let me get on with my life." I gulped between sobs. "I'd be better off without you." All the emotion of my roller-coaster weeks with Kai, leading up to last Friday's kiss, had finally welled to the surface like an erupting volcano.

"Don't cry," he said, gently wiping at the tears on

136

my cheek. "Please don't cry, Kirstie. Let me explain. I thought I was skating pairs to kill time . . . until something better came along." He sat me down on a bleacher. "But now everything's changed. I don't want to stop skating." His clear blue eyes were staring down into mine. "I want to stay here with you."

"That's not what you said to your friends."

A smile crossed his face then. "Give me a break, Kirsten. Can you imagine me telling those hockey heads that I like figure skating? I do have an image to live up to, you know."

"I don't know," I said, wiping away the tears with the back of my hand. "I don't know anything about you. . . ."

"You know how amazing it was to kiss me."

He thought that kiss was incredible too?

"I drove around in my car for hours that night. I told myself I couldn't possibly let myself get involved with you." He smiled at me, and I couldn't help but notice how handsome he was when his eyes crinkled at the sides.

"I didn't think there was any future in it, knowing how you felt about me. That you hated my guts. . . ."

"I don't hate you anymore," I said. It came out barely more than a whisper. "I didn't want to like you, Kai. You've bugged the heck out of me since the day we met. But I can't help myself. And that kiss . . . well, I wasn't ready for the way it made me feel either."

"How did it make you feel?"

"Like I've never felt before."

He took my cold hands in his strong, warm ones. "Me too," he said. "Just like the first time we skated together to the music . . . almost as if there were some magical spell over us."

I nodded. "That's exactly how I felt."

"If it's a magic spell," he said softly, moving closer . . . so close I could feel his warm breath on my face when he spoke, "I don't want it to break, do you?"

I shook my head. I was finding it hard to speak with Kai's lips so near mine and the warm current from his hands running up my arms.

"Kai? Kirsten? Where have you run off to now?" Vlad's booming voice echoed across the rink. The spell was broken. "No goofing off in the middle of practice. I want you out here right now."

Kai squeezed my hands. "I'll be right back," he whispered. "Don't go anywhere."

But Vlad was already headed our way. "What's going on?" he demanded. "Why aren't you out on the ice?"

"Kirsten's upset," Kai explained. "I'd like to take her home."

"Upset? Over what? Have you been annoying her again?" Vlad accused.

"I'm okay now." I stood up, sniffing back the last of my tears. "I'm just fine."

"By my watch, you have twenty more minutes of practice time." Vlad was staring at me, trying to guess what had been going on. He must have thought Kai and I had been in a fight. It was obvious that I'd been crying.

"Couldn't you let us off early just this once?" Kai begged. "We did stay extra late on Friday to nail the death spiral."

"And do you know that Kirsten wants you to drive her home?"

I nodded. "I'd like him to."

A smile crossed Vlad's face. "Huh!" he said loudly, slapping his big hand against his thigh. "My instincts are never wrong!"

"What are you talking about, Coach?" Kai asked.

"I was right, wasn't I?" he said. "Chemistry. It never fails. Okay, go, little ones. With my blessing." He shooed us away. "But be here on time in the morning."

Then he waddled back to the rink, leaving Kai and me staring at each other.

"He turned into a pussycat," I said.

Kai was grinning. "He's pleased at being right about you and me," he said. "He knew we'd hit it off from the very beginning. That's why he wanted us to skate together."

"I don't know what made him think that you and I would ever get along," I said. "All we did was fight. You have to admit you were a major pain." I grinned at him.

"And you have to admit you acted like Queen of the Rink," Kai countered. Then he paused. "I know I haven't been easy to deal with. I guess I was mad at the world for a while there—angry at

139

myself, mainly. And pairs skating was the last thing I wanted to do."

"And now?" I whispered.

"Now I have the feeling it's going to be okay," he said. He touched my arm. "Go get changed, and I'll drive you home."

TWELVE

I RAN INTO the locker room, threw off my skates, and pulled on my sweatshirt and jeans. I brushed my hair in front of the mirror and wished I'd brought some makeup with me. Then I called my parents from the pay phone to tell them I'd be late and headed for the door.

There was no way I could have missed Kai or his beat-up old Camaro. It was black, with fire decals down both sides. And the deafening sound outside the rink was a combination of the engine revving and the smoke belching out of the tailpipe.

"So you do exist outside the rink," I said as I hopped into the passenger's seat. "This is the first time I'm seeing you without your skates on."

"Well, what do you think? Am I even better without my skates?" he teased.

I wasn't sure how to answer him. Now that I was alone with Kai, I found it impossible to think straight. "Will this thing make it to a restaurant?" I asked, deciding to change the subject. "I'm starved."

Kai took off, the tires screeching behind us. "No problem. This baby has taken me to Squaw Valley and back zillions of times. That was when I used to have time to ski."

"I love skiing."

"Let's go when we win Western Qualifyings!"

"*If* we win Westerns, we'll be preparing for Nationals. We can't risk getting hurt."

"But life's all about taking risks," he said.

After we had turned out of the parking lot, Kai pushed the gas pedal to the floor. Suddenly streetlights flashed past in a blur of speed.

"Just don't take too many risks with me in the car!" I warned, gripping the armrest.

He laughed. "Don't worry. I'm a great driver. I love moving fast. When I become famous and make my first million, the first thing I'll do is buy an expensive sports car. A Ferrari, probably."

"Well, you can't drive this old heap like a Ferrari," I said. "I'd like to get to dinner in one piece, please."

I heard him sigh as he slowed to a normal speed.

"If you want to do something, you should do it all the way. Nothing's worth doing if it's not fun. That's my philosophy."

"Did hockey stop being fun for you?" I asked quietly. "Is that why you quit?"

"I loved hockey. I'll always love hockey. I just can't play anymore."

142

"Why not?"

"I'm just not ready to talk about it. Hockey is history, okay? Let's drop it."

"Okay," I said, taking a deep breath. But before the night was through, I was determined to find out the truth.

We were heading up the freeway in the direction of San Francisco. Skyscrapers lit up the skyline as we came around Hospital Curve.

"We're eating in the city? That's great." I turned in my seat to face him. I took a close look at his light brown good looks. I liked the way his eyes sparkled when he smiled . . . the way one wisp of hair always threatened to fall in his eye.

We came down from the freeway, crossed through the financial district, and turned into a maze of little back streets. I had totally lost track of where we were.

"Are you sure you know where you're going?" I asked cautiously as we turned into an alley.

"Trust me," Kai said.

"You really think I should?" I teased.

He nodded. "I really think you should," he said quietly. "Anyway, you don't have a choice right now." Then he eased the Camaro into a space between two garbage cans. "Let's leave the car here," he said.

"Here?" I could hear my voice tremble. Where was Kai taking me? This didn't look like a restaurant district. My heart raced with fear. This wasn't another joke, was it?

Kai gallantly held out his hand to me as I cautiously opened the car door. "Follow me," he encouraged as we set off down the alley.

At the end of the alley Kai led me up a flight of steps. I was afraid he was leading me to a smoky nightclub, so I was pleasantly surprised when he pushed open a big red door with a carved dragon. We were inside a Chinese restaurant. At least I thought it was a Chinese restaurant. It smelled great, but I didn't see any tables. The entire place was filled with tiny booths that looked like changing cubicles at a public swimming pool.

Just then a hostess signaled for us to follow her. She opened the door to one of the booths and stood back for us to enter. Inside was a table and chairs. She closed the door again. We were completely alone.

"Isn't this neat?" Kai asked, leaning over to touch my hand. Kai held my hand for nearly five hours every day, but somehow this time felt different. Was it the delicious smells wafting into our private room . . . or the fact that my hands weren't freezing for once? It didn't matter, though. Because I liked it no matter what the reason.

A waiter came in with tea and menus. The menu was written in Chinese characters on one side of the page and English on the other. Kai pointed impressively to the Chinese side of the page. "We'll have one of those, one of these, and one of these," he said with an air of confidence.

"Very good, sir," the waiter said, bowing as he left us alone in our room.

"You sure know your way around Chinese food," I said. "I'm impressed. I didn't know you could read Chinese."

He grinned conspiratorially. "I'll let you in on a little secret. I just closed my eyes and pointed. I can't wait to see what turns up."

"Kai? What if it's something really ` weird? What if we get bird's nests and shark fins?"

"Lighten up, Kirstie. Think of it as an experience." He leaned back in his seat. "When you're with me, you've got to learn to live dangerously."

"I've been living dangerously, six feet above the ice, since I first met you."

"And it's been fun, hasn't it?" he asked seriously. His eyes were looking straight into mine.

"Some of it," I admitted, glancing nervously at Kai.

The first dish arrived—a huge mound of slender, transparent noodles. Kai picked up some with his chopsticks and put it into his mouth. I imitated him as I tasted the crunchy, slightly salty food.

"These noodles are pretty good," he said to the waiter as the man placed a dish of thinly sliced meat in front of us.

"That's not noodle. That's jellyfish," the waiter said.

"Jellyfish!" I spat out what was left in my mouth and wiped my tongue with my linen napkin.

Kai just smiled, delighted. As soon as the waiter left us again, Kai laughed out loud. "I can't believe we're eating jellyfish, Kirsten. I wonder what other yummy treats we've got here."

"You can be head food taster," I offered. "If you eat something and don't throw up, maybe I'll try it."

"Gee, thanks a lot."

"You ordered this stuff," I reminded him.

"Okay. I'm not a chicken. Watch me. I'm about to taste this meat now. See?" Kai put some beef into his mouth. Then his eyes opened very wide and he made coughing sounds.

"What?" I asked, alarmed. "What is it?"

Kai held his throat and groaned.

"Kai! What's the matter?"

"Nothing. It's delicious. Psych!" He almost did choke then because he was laughing so hard. Then he picked up a big, plump shrimp in his chopsticks and fed it to me. And I felt myself blushing. I liked being with Kai. He knew how to make me feel special . . . and that was something I really needed to feel at that moment. I had been through so much in the past few days, I was beginning to feel almost beaten up.

I quickly tried to pick up another bite of shrimp with my chopsticks, but I couldn't do it. "Can you show me how to do this, Kai? Please."

"Simple," he said. "First you place your chopsticks like this." He placed the chopsticks in my hand, and I relaxed in his gentle touch. "Then you open and close them this way." He demonstrated. I couldn't pull my eyes from his intense gaze. "Now pick up a piece of spring roll, carefully dip it into the soy sauce, and . . ." As he slowly lifted the food to his mouth, I felt my lips yearn to touch his. To feel those warm lips on mine again. Then just as he was about to take a bite, the spring roll slipped from his chopsticks and dropped onto his lap.

"Ouch, that thing is hot!" he exclaimed, retrieving it quickly.

"Nice demonstration," I said, taking a quick breath. "Would you mind doing it again? I didn't quite get the last part," I joked, hoping he wouldn't see the flush on my cheeks.

He made a face. "I don't know what went wrong. Usually I'm an expert with chopsticks. Okay, here's how it's done." He picked up the biggest shrimp with his chopsticks, moved it toward his lips, and . . . it fell straight into his tea and splashed onto his sweatshirt.

Without missing a beat he looked at me seriously. "Of course, real connoisseurs of Chinese food always wash their shrimp in tea before they eat it." Kai's eyes seemed to dance with amusement.

I watched as Kai served himself more beef—with a fork this time. He was so different from all the guys I knew. He wasn't afraid to take a chance, to make a fool of himself. It was as if I were seeing Kai for the first time . . . really seeing him for the person he was inside. And I liked what I saw. Tonight Kai wasn't the stuck-up hockey jock who thought he was too cool to be a pairs skater. He was a sweet, sensitive young man.

The intimacy of the private room gave me the courage to dig deeper. "Kai, what really happened with your hockey career?" I wanted to know everything about him.

There wasn't a sound in the booth as Kai looked down at his plate, and then he began. "I don't know what you've already heard."

"There was some kind of accident at the hockey rink."

"Yeah, an accident, but not to me," he explained, looking straight at me. "I was a pretty good hockey player. Actually I was one of the best," he said without any of the typical Kai swagger. "But one particular day, I was having a bad game. You know, the kind of day when you can't do anything right?"

I nodded. Boy, did I know about those kinds of days.

"I missed every shot I took. And there was this guy on the other team with a big mouth. Every time I messed up, he had some rude comment. You know the kind of thing. 'You think you're so hot, Bergstrom. How come you keep missing, huh? You're totally lame. Do you need glasses? What a wimp. . . .'" Kai made a face as he mimicked the guy.

"He kept it up all through the game. I was getting angrier and angrier. And then my chance came. We went after the puck and reached the barrier at the same moment. I bodychecked him—used my body to slam him into the barrier. Hockey players do it all the time.

"Boy, did I bodycheck him. I slammed him against that barrier with all my strength. 'Still think I'm a wimp, buddy?' I whispered in his ear.

But the guy just looked at me, then he shook his head and he slid to the ice.

"Don't get me wrong. Bodychecking is allowed." Kai looked down. "I did everything the coach had taught me to do. I didn't expect the barrier to catch the guy the wrong way. I didn't want to break his ribs, puncture his lung. . . ."

"Oh, Kai, that's terrible," I said, reaching out to touch him. I was amazed at the tension in his usually relaxed hands.

He nodded. "For a while they thought he might die. He recovered, but he'll never play hockey again. And I . . . I'll never play hockey again either." Kai pulled away from me.

"Why not? It wasn't your fault."

He shook his head. "It doesn't matter. I nearly killed someone, Kirsten. I was suspended for unsportsmanlike conduct. Everyone at the rink blamed me for what happened. They all thought I'd done it on purpose . . . and deep down I couldn't stop wondering the same thing." This time Kai reached out to take my hand. "Had I really meant to hurt him so badly? So I left the team and never went back.

"The guys were all very nice about it. They came to my house, said that accidents happened. And they asked me to come back. But I couldn't."

"Why not? It was just a freak accident, Kai."

He looked down at our hands and spoke very slowly. "Because I was afraid I might get that

149

angry again, that I might kill someone next time. I knew I had the power to hurt someone, Kirsten. I couldn't handle that."

There was a long silence. "I know I've been impossible to be around," he said at last. "I've been so angry, so frustrated. My entire life had been all planned out, and then suddenly I didn't know what I wanted anymore. Can you forgive me for being such a pain?"

"Of course I forgive you," I said, squeezing his hands in mine. "But you have to learn to forgive yourself, Kai. You can't undo what happened, but you can put it behind you and get on with your life. You can enjoy skating again and look forward to the future."

He looked at me, his eyes bright with hope. "I think I'm learning to do that," he said. "Pairs-skating champion isn't such a bad title, is it?"

"Are you kidding? I can't imagine what could be better."

"I'm glad you couldn't do that triple jump, Kirsten Hayes," he said in a husky voice. "Or we might never have skated together." He looked at me with concern. "Do you miss being a singles skater?"

I smiled at him tenderly. "Solo skaters don't get to fly through the air, six feet above the ice. It's the most incredible feeling, Kai. And they don't get to land in your arms either."

Kai came around the table to sit next to me. He moved close . . . very close. And his lips were mere inches from mine as he whispered, "I'm so glad we came here tonight. I can't even remember why I waited so long to tell you . . ." But he didn't finish his thought.

Suddenly our lips came together for an earth-shattering kiss. Kai's lips were warm and demanding as they crushed against mine.

I can't tell you how long we stayed in that private little room, talking and laughing and kissing each other. I learned so much about Kai that night. We both opened up for the first time. I even told him about my breakup with Troy.

The day had begun as one of the worst days I'd ever had. Yet it had become the greatest day of my life. The day I began to fall in love with Kai.

THIRTEEN

TUESDAY WAS UNBEARABLE and amazing at the same time. School was impossible to deal with. Between the whispers and stares as I walked through the familiar halls to the tension I felt every time Troy or one of his loud teammates passed by, I thought I might explode. It was obvious that word had gotten out about Troy and me splitting up. And I wasn't surprised to find flighty Tanya Schmid giggling with Troy in front of his locker before lunch. She certainly hadn't wasted any time. And neither had I, I realized. Normally a scene like that would have upset me. But this was no normal week. This was the week that everything I'd ever wanted began to come true.

Things between me and Kai that morning couldn't have been better. We were now in total sync on—and off—the ice. Tuesday afternoon I stood along the side of the rink and did some stretches. The ice looked brand-new, as if the Zamboni had just cleaned it. I was the first skater on the ice. The rink was quiet. Very few lights were on and shadows covered the ice. As I finished my warm-ups with a high jump, the scraping sound of my skates echoed in the empty arena. Out of the corner of my eye I noticed another skater stepping onto the ice. Kai.

He looked more confident and casual than any other high-school guy I knew. He was wearing a pair of worn gray sweats and a dark blue sweatshirt. And he looked even better than usual.

Kai held out his hand and silently led me to the center of the ice. His hand was warm and dry and sure, and I felt safe . . . secure . . . on the ice with him. Hands still linked, we skated in perfect unison around one end of the rink.

"You're beautiful, Kirsten," Kai whispered as we came close together.

I just smiled and blushed. I wasn't used to the new Kai, the kinder, gentler Kai. To cover my embarrassment, I laughed and said, "Thanks."

Kai paused to peel off his blue sweatshirt. Underneath he had on a gray long-sleeve T-shirt. Kai tossed his sweatshirt into the stands, then took my hands again.

"Together we can do anything," he said as we skated backward, picking up speed.

As I moved along with him I found his confidence contagious. "You know, Kai, I think you might be right." And I really meant it.

Since we'd begun skating together, we'd made tremendous progress. In the beginning I found it hard to get used to skating with someone . . . to get used to Kai's bad attitude. But now it felt so natural. Actually I couldn't imagine skating alone again. Half of me would feel as if it were missing.

"Of course, I'm right," Kai said as we prepared for our press lift. "And we'll prove it to the judges at Sectionals."

I landed effortlessly on the ice and skated smoothly into my favorite dance steps. It all happened so naturally, so perfectly. I couldn't hold back my smile.

From the squeeze of Kai's hand, I knew he thought so too.

"Hi, Kirsten," Alice called out as she skated up to me Wednesday morning. She was wearing an amazing hot pink unitard with a dramatic electric purple stripe.

Kai and I had just finished a dry run-through of our routine and I was taking a quick break.

"Hey, Alice. You looked great out there." Alice was so graceful and strong. And I had seen her consistently nail her triples time and time again.

"You've got to be kidding," she said, wiping ice off the bottom of her skates. "I'm so uptight about the competition. I just saw the poster for Sectionals in the hall, and now I'm in a total panic. I'm afraid I'm about to snap from the tension."

"Yoo-hoo, Alice, honey," came an annoyingly familiar voice.

"That woman just doesn't know how to listen," Alice said, looking angrily toward the voice. "Vlad told her not to come to practice, but here she is." Alice really did seem as if she were about to crack.

I watched as Vlad tapped Alice and the two of them walked toward Ms. Attwood. They began arguing, but not loud enough for me to hear. After a few moments Vlad shrugged and turned away, his mouth set in a hard line.

"Aren't you glad you don't have parents like that?" Kai snuck up on me and kissed my ear as he whispered into it.

I giggled from the ticklish sensation his kiss sent through my head. "Yeah, competitive skating is hard enough without the pressure Alice gets from her mother."

Kai seemed surprised. "You don't really think we'll be under a lot of pressure, do you? I can't wait to wow them at Sectionals. I used to love the crowd at hockey games."

"You just love when you're the center of attention," I teased.

"As long as I'm the center of your attention, I know I can do no wrong."

The Pacific Coast Sectionals was all anyone could talk about for the rest of the week. And when I saw the official poster hanging in the hall between the locker rooms, I felt a special thrill shiver through me. PACIFIC COAST SECTIONALS. JANUARY 10–12.

By January 12, Kai and I would be headed for Nationals!

But Thursday afternoon everything seemed to change. Kai was back to his moody self, and we skated like amateurs that day. Moves that had been so simple . . . so magical only a few days before suddenly seemed impossible.

When Kai dropped me the third time in a row, I angrily turned on him. "What's going on, Kai?" I demanded. "If this keeps up, I won't have an inch of me that isn't black and blue. It almost feels as if you're dropping me on purpose."

"Get real, Kirsten." He helped me up off the ice. "Why would I drop you on purpose? It takes two to do lifts, you know?"

"What are you saying, Kai? Are you suggesting it's my fault that I'm spending so much time sitting on the ice today?" I brushed ice off my aching legs and looked him straight in the eye.

Something was different about Kai today. Gone was the confident, sure guy who I had fallen for. In his place was the angry, frightened Kai I had first met so many weeks before. What had happened between Monday night's perfection and today's misery? Why the sudden change?

But Kai didn't give me a chance to find out.

"If the blame fits . . . ," he said as he skated off the ice.

★   ★   ★

Friday morning Kai showed up at the *end* of practice. Vlad had been furious all morning, and he'd made me work on my spins and jumps as we waited . . . and waited for Kai to appear.

The moment I saw Kai, standing in his jeans and brown leather jacket, I knew something was wrong—very wrong.

Kai motioned for me to join him off the ice. "Kirsten, I need to talk to you."

I skated to the entrance to the rink, then stepped onto the rubber matting and sat on the bleachers. "So talk."

"I've been up all night thinking," Kai said as he paced back and forth in front of me. "There's no easy way to say this, but . . . well, Kirsten, I'm really sorry, but I don't think I can do this anymore. Figure skating just isn't my thing." He took off his jacket, threw it onto the bleacher next to me, and continued pacing. "I've tried and I've tried, but ultimately it's not my kind of sport. I can't compete in the Sectionals. I won't. I'm sorry if I let you down. . . ."

I opened my mouth, ready for a fight, but I couldn't make any words come out. I just stared at him, dumbfounded, for a minute. "What . . . what are you talking about?" I finally stammered.

"I've changed my mind," he said, sounding stronger now. "You probably have enough time to find a new partner. You're such a great skater, I'm sure Vlad can find you someone who's better than I am."

"So you're quitting? You're walking out on me now?"

"I don't have a choice." He stopped moving. "I don't want to compete and that's final. And you can't make me skate."

White-hot anger flared up inside me. "I trusted you, Kai!" I yelled, and I didn't care who heard me. "And now you're chickening out? What's the deal—have you decided that you're too cool to skate pairs? What about taking risks? I thought that was what life was all about. Those were your words, Kai, not mine." I was really burning now. "Did your hockey pals get to you? I thought you were tougher than that. What about me? What about us? Don't we count at all?"

"Of course we count," he said. "It's just that—don't ask me to enter this competition, Kirsten."

"Why?" I demanded, tears stinging at my cheeks. "Anytime something goes wrong in your life, you just clam up and run away. Why won't you tell me the truth? Don't I deserve to know why you're breaking my heart?"

"There's no point," he said bitterly. "This is just something I know I can't handle."

"I thought you were Mr. Cool, the guy who never gets nervous in front of a crowd!" I yelled. "I don't know what's going on here, but you made a commitment, buddy. You're not just letting yourself down—you're letting me down too. I guess I was wrong when I thought I'd found

158

somebody special. You're just like every other guy. When it comes down to the wire, you only look out for number one. Boy, was I a fool. And to think I was falling in love with you."

He stepped toward me then and put out his arms as if he were going to hold my shoulders. "Kirsten, listen, I . . ."

But I didn't wait to hear his lame excuses. I ran toward the locker room and broke down and cried.

FOURTEEN

VLAD HAD SUGGESTED I take a day or two off. I should talk to my parents, think about what I'd like to do about the situation with Kai, and let him know my decision when I was ready.

What were my choices? Choice *A* was to go back to solo skating—but I knew I'd never nail the triple toe loop. And without that jump I'd never get my chance at the gold.

Weeks of working at pairs had made me stronger at the things I was naturally good at—spins, footwork, and the more emotional, lyrical moves. But my jumps hadn't improved at all. And I didn't want to go back to singles. It would be so lonely skating without Kai now . . . as if half of me were missing. It would feel horrible to do a great flying camel without Kai spinning right beside me.

Choice *B* wasn't any better, though. *B* was to find another partner, hope we click, skate our butts off, and pray there was enough time to prepare for Sectionals—which I knew there wasn't.

How could Kai have done this to me? He didn't only break our shot at competing . . . but he also broke my heart.

By Saturday night I was a total mess. I was angry and depressed at the same time. I had spent the entire day curled up on my bed, waiting for inspiration to strike. It had been one day, nine hours, and thirty-seven minutes since Kai had skated out of my life. And I had finally come to accept that there was absolutely nothing I could do about it.

I glanced around my room. Everywhere I looked, I saw something related to skating: trophies, dirty sweatshirts, wool tights hanging on the back of my desk chair, posters on the walls, my skating bag, and a clump of colorful laces on my desk. Immediately tears welled in my eyes. I had never felt such utter hopelessness before. I took the piece of paper on which I had tried writing an English essay that was due Monday morning and crumpled it up, throwing it into the growing pile in the corner of my room.

Without Kai nothing worked, nothing mattered. And what hurt most was the fact that he hadn't trusted me enough to tell me what was really wrong.

I don't know how long I stayed there crying. I probably would have fallen asleep that way if I hadn't been startled by the doorbell ringing downstairs. I heard muffled voices, then footsteps to my bedroom door.

"Kirsten," Mom called softly. "There's someone here to see you."

I quickly wiped away my tears. I was wearing a T-shirt, so I threw on a pair of jeans and slowly made my way to the door.

"Hi," Kai said softly, a hesitant smile across his lips. "I hope you don't mind that I'm here. I was just driving around and I had to come over. I made a mistake, Kirsten."

"That's an understatement," I said quietly as my mom turned to go back downstairs. Kai and I were standing outside my bedroom door. It was strange to be so close to him in my house. It was too intimate. I couldn't handle my runaway emotions with my family in hearing range. "Let's go outside."

I closed the front door quietly behind me. We walked across to the big plum tree in the backyard and sat down together. Below us the lights of San Francisco twinkled on the other side of the Bay as a ribbon of fog came to swallow them up.

"You were right." Kai was staring out at the sky. "I do clam up and run away when something bad happens. This is hard for me," he said. "My dad is an ex-army guy. Be a man and don't show your feelings—that's how I was raised. Don't cry—you're a boy."

It was odd, but Kai and I had never talked about our families before. We hadn't gotten the

162

chance. We had only realized we'd liked each other a few days before Kai had ruined my life.

"I learned to shut up when something bothered me," he continued. "And when I was hurting inside, I acted like I didn't care. That's why I was so impossible when you first met me." He looked at me cautiously, as if I were a wild animal who might jump up and bite him.

"I'm sorry, Kirsten. I'm really, truly sorry . . . ," Kai started, then his voice trailed off. He took a deep breath. "I realized something today. For the first time in my life I care about someone else more than myself. I hurt you, Kirsten, and I'll do anything in the world to make it up to you."

"I don't understand, Kai," I said huskily. "You still haven't explained what made you quit. What made you walk out on me."

"There was a poster in the hallway," Kai said.

"For Sectionals. I saw it."

"It also said that Nationals are at my old rink in San Jose," he said hesitantly.

"So?"

He looked at me as if I were completely clueless. "Kirstie, you have to understand. I can't go back there and skate pairs."

"All this is because you don't want to go back to a rink where an accident happened a year ago?"

"It wasn't just any accident. I nearly killed a person. They hate my guts at that rink."

"Kai, you're making such a big thing out of nothing," I said. "Whatever happened in that

163

hockey game is over and forgotten. Even your teammates told you they want you back."

He shook his head. "You don't know what it was like—the way people looked at me. The whispers behind my back. Everyone thought I'd done it on purpose—at least the officials did or they wouldn't have suspended me. I felt like a criminal. I can't face those people again."

We sat there, staring out into darkness. The fog had now enveloped the lights. And the mournful sound of a foghorn echoed from Bay Bridge.

"You can't let this one incident destroy your whole life." I reached over to hold his hand. "I'm not thinking about myself right now, about what will happen to me if we don't skate together. You're a supertalented skater, Kai. Are you willing to give up a shot at the big time just because some people in San Jose might whisper about you?"

He was silent for a while, then he said, "When you put it that way, it does sound pretty dumb."

"As long as you know you didn't hurt that guy on purpose, who cares what other people think?"

He looked at me and nodded seriously, his hand still in mine. "I guess you're right."

I put my other hand on his arm. "Besides, if you're going to get anywhere as a skater, you'll have to get used to being judged unfairly sometimes. And other skaters always say catty things, trying to psych each other out. It's part of competition. You just have to learn to smile. And don't ever let them see that they're bugging you. Because then they've won."

Kai covered my hand with his own. "I miss you, Kirsten. I miss skating with you."

I took a long time before saying anything. "I miss you too." I paused again. "Does this mean you want to skate with me again?"

"Yes, Kirsten. If you'll let me."

"You're my partner, Kai, and we're going to win the Pacific Coast Sectionals. Nothing else matters."

"You're wrong. Something else does," he said softly.

I looked up at him, a bit confused.

"Me and you," he said. "We matter. I think it was fate that made you bump into me that day."

His eyes were gazing warmly into mine. No longer did they shoot angry ice blue fire. They were softer now and they glowed with tenderness. I moved closer to get a better look and was overwhelmed by Kai's warm, sweet breath as we sealed our reunion with a tender kiss.

FIFTEEN

K AI AND I were listed as one of the first to
skate in our short program. As a new team
we were low in the rankings. The better-known
pairs performed later in the day.

We were standing in front of the ice rink to
the left of the lobby. There were two Olympic-
size ice rinks in the arena, one on each side of the
locker rooms. Kai explained that one rink was for
hockey and the other for figures.

The rink looked ten times more beautiful
than our rink in San Mateo. The ice looked
brand-new, as if a Zamboni had just cleaned it,
and the lighting was mostly natural—unlike the
fluorescent lighting we were used to. The sky-
lights in the ceiling let in the California sunshine.
And there were flags from all over the world
hanging around the rink.

I had never seen such an amazing rink. Just

looking at it made me want to skate my best.

I grabbed Vlad's arm as he studied the program. "How does it look, Vlad?"

"Not bad," he said, nodding thoughtfully. "Of course it is an obstacle to skate so early, but it can also work to your advantage. The judges won't be worn out when you skate. They'll be fresh and ready for you to make them sit up and say, Wow!"

"I hope so," I said, looking at Kai. I was beginning to feel nervous now that we were there. Kai had been quiet all morning. I wondered if he was nervous too.

"Your short program is easy for you," Vlad continued. "And it is fun to watch. You'll make the judges smile. Go out there and have fun."

"Easy for him to say," Kai said, gripping my hand as if it were a lifeline.

We glided onto the ice, taking long, fluid strokes to warm up. I leaned into my skating leg and pushed off with my free leg, slowly building to Kai's speed. We silently circled the rink several times, gaining more power with each trip around. Then I did a quick run and began skating backward. I crossed one foot over the other until I was facing Kai. He seemed tense, stiffer than I'd ever seen him before.

"Breathe, Kai," I whispered. I needed to loosen him up, take his mind off the fact that his hockey buddies could appear at any moment. "Deep breaths—focus on me. Imagine we're skating all alone on a pond in the middle of the mountains. It's just the two of us. Stay calm and focus." The skirt of my workout clothes billowed in the breeze, and I felt my own body begin to relax as we performed familiar motions.

After warm-ups we split apart to change into our short-program costumes. This was our robot-coming-to-life number, and we wore silver metallic outfits designed by a woman in Berkeley. They were very startling—eye-catching. I noticed the other girls in more conventional costumes, staring at me.

"What are you supposed to be?" one of them asked.

"A robot," I said smugly. I wasn't about to let that girl psych me out. I watched her smirk to a friend.

Wait until you see me and Kai together on the ice, I thought. *We'll see who's smirking then.*

"I've never seen you around," another of the girls in the locker room said. "Are you new to this?"

"Yes. It's my first competition," I said. *In pairs skating,* I added silently, grinning to myself.

"Don't get too nervous. It's fun," the girl added. "I'm sure you'll do just fine. Don't worry too much about falling on your jumps."

I knew she was trying to psych me out by putting that thought into my mind. A lot of skating happens in your mind. You have to visualize—imagine yourself nailing a jump, a spin, a lift—before you could perform it. So if you had a vision of falling every time you attempted a jump, you were almost guaranteed to miss it. It was a nasty trick, but I was prepared. I wouldn't let anything stop me—nothing!

"Oh, I'm not nervous." I was tempted to make some comment about Nationals last year. No one skating at the Pacific Coast Sectionals had made it to Nationals yet. No one but me. But I kept my mouth shut. It would be more fun to blow them away on the ice.

I gave my hair one last coating of spray gel and went out to meet Kai. He was sitting on a bench in the waiting area, along with some other skaters.

"My fellow robot!" I called. "I hope your circuits are all working well."

He managed a tight smile, but he still seemed very tense.

"Have you seen how many people are out there?" Kai gestured with his right arm, sweeping it around the rink.

"You told me you loved skating in front of a crowd!"

"Yeah, but not this crowd. I know I'll freak out if I see a face I recognize."

"Think mountain pond, Kai," I whispered in his ear just before I kissed him for luck. "You'll be fine. The moment the music starts, you'll forget about everything except what comes next in our program. And if one of us does screw up or falls, don't think about it. Switch off right away and go on to the next move. Got it?"

"Yes, ma'am," he said. Then he squeezed my hand. "Don't worry. I won't let you down."

Suddenly the rink announcer called for the first couple to step onto the ice. They were very young, a couple of kids from Oregon. And they seemed nervous. As the girl fell for the seventh time I couldn't help but feel sorry for them. I quickly looked over at Kai, his pale face a mask. I knew he was afraid we might end up like that first couple.

The first team scored in the high threes. Six was a perfect score, and you needed midfives to be in the running for a medal.

The next pair was better, but their skating lacked emotion. All their marks were low fours.

We were next. Before we stepped onto the ice, I grabbed both of Kai's hands and looked him straight in the eyes. "Remember, deep breaths," I said as we both sucked in air. I exhaled, then said, "Focus on me . . . on us. We're gonna blow these people away!"

Kai's hand shook as we stepped onto the ice. I hoped once the roar of the crowd died down and the opening chords of our music began, Kai would relax and enjoy our moment in the spotlight.

When the music began, we were at the center of the ice. We slowly went into our robot moves, skating backward, away from each other. So far, so good. Then came the time for our side-by-side axels. Our preparation was strong, but Kai teetered on the landing and almost lost his balance. Thankfully he was strong enough to right himself before he fell. I smiled as he grabbed my hand. Next was a combination spin and then side-by-side footwork. . . . One by one we nailed all the required elements.

Our skating was technically perfect, but I couldn't feel the usual emotion Kai and I had when we skated together. Instead I found myself picking up on his nervousness. If only we could have done our free skate first—that was when we really clicked together. Too much of our short program was apart and we lacked all emotional involvement.

We finally finished to loud applause. But I wasn't at all sure how well we had done. Kai and I skated to the side of the rink where Vlad had watched us and stood there, waiting for our marks. Five-three, five-four . . . so far they were better than I had hoped. Five-five, five-three . . . all in the midfives.

"You did well," Vlad cheered, putting an arm around both our shoulders. "A little tense, which the judges noticed, but all the elements were there. If you place in the top seven, I think you have a real chance."

Now we just had to watch the other performers and wait, all the time praying that no other team would do much better.

I put on a sweatshirt, jacket, and pair of sweatpants over my costume to keep warm. Then Kai and I made our way to the top of the bleachers. That way we could get a good view of the competition. Most of the other couples looked good, but a few completely blew it by falling or getting out of sync.

Suddenly I looked up as someone sat beside us. I had assumed it was Vlad, coming to prepare us for the long program. But it wasn't Vlad. It was a dark-haired guy in a Sharks hockey jacket.

"Hi, Kai, how's it going?" he asked.

"Jeff! What's up? What are you doing here?" Kai exclaimed. Kai turned to me. "This is Jeff Bateman. He was on my old hockey team—one of the best players."

"*The* best player since you left," Jeff said, laughing.

"Don't tell me you came to watch a figure-skating competition?" Kai asked.

"Not exactly," Jeff explained. "But I saw you guys out there. You were awesome. I can't believe how quickly you learned a new sport. But there never was anything you couldn't do on skates, Bergstrom." He leaned closer to Kai. "Actually I'm here to see Tommy Reiley. He's at the rink today."

"Tommy Reiley? The Boston College hockey coach?" Kai seemed suddenly excited . . . too excited.

"Yeah, and I hear he's anxious to give away some scholarships. I've got an appointment with him in ten minutes."

"Good for you, buddy. Go for it!" Kai slapped him on the shoulders.

Jeff looked at him seriously. "Why don't you come with me?"

"Me?" Kai's brow cringed.

"Come on, Kai. You know every college team would have fought to sign you up if that accident hadn't happened. At least come and talk to Coach Reiley. Maybe he'll invite you to Boston to try out," Jeff tempted. "If I remember correctly, you always wanted to go to Boston College, didn't you?"

"Yeah, but . . . I haven't played hockey for nearly a year now, Jeff."

"So what? You made high-school all-American, didn't you? Reiley knows who you are." He grabbed Kai's arm. "Kai, this is your big chance to put all that dumb stuff behind you. You had a bad break. This can make up for it. You and a college coach. One-on-one. What more could you ask?"

Kai had yet to look at me. It was as if I had disappeared. I cleared my throat.

"Well, um . . . Kirsten and I have to get ready for our long program. . . . ," Kai began.

"That's not for another couple of hours," Jeff pointed out. "At least come and talk to him. What have you got to lose?"

Kai got to his feet. "I guess I would like to meet him. He's always been a hero of mine." He finally turned to me. "I'll be back in a little while, Kirsten. Don't go away, okay?"

He didn't give me time to say no as he charged down the stairs. I felt cold and scared as I wrapped my jacket around me, hugging my arms to myself. I couldn't believe it. That stupid coach would probably offer Kai a scholarship to play hockey.

And of course Kai would accept it. How could he refuse? He'd always said that pairs wasn't his dream. He wanted to be a hockey star, and now he might get his shot. I knew I couldn't stand in Kai's way. He loved hockey. If that was what he really wanted to do, then he deserved this chance.

When Kai returned to the bleachers, I pretended to study the program in my hand. I was afraid to look at his light brown hair or his perfect smile for fear that I might break down and beg him to stay with me.

"Hi," he said, sliding into the seat beside me.

"Hi. How was the college coach?" I choked out.

"He's a nice guy," Kai said. "I'm glad I got a chance to meet him."

"Did . . . did he know who you were?" I stammered. *Get ahold of yourself, Kirsten.*

"Yeah, he did. I was totally amazed."

"Did he offer you a scholarship or anything. . . ."

"Yes, he did," Kai said. "Actually, he almost came out and offered me a free ride. He wants me to go up to Boston for a weekend and work out with the team."

"Kai, that's great . . . ," I managed to say. But I didn't sound very enthused. "If that's what you really want."

"I told him thanks, but no thanks."

"You did?" I snuck a glance at him.

He was smiling. "I told him it was more fun throwing you around the ice." Then he got serious. "You didn't think I'd leave you, did you?"

"I was afraid you might. I know hockey is your first love."

"Correction, hockey *was* my first love," he said. "I can't look back, Kirstie. I've got a new love now, and skating is only a part of it."

"You mean it?" I knew my eyes were shining. I felt a great rush of happiness well up inside me.

"I mean it. Now let's go ace that long program, blow those judges away!"

I was in the girls' locker room, changing into my flowing dark blue freestyle costume. My mom helped me adjust my blue sequined cap. I was afraid it might fall off during the death spiral. Then she used the curling iron to give my long hair a bit of a curl. When she was finished, I didn't recognize the elegant stranger looking back at me in the mirror.

I turned my head and smiled at a familiar face I saw heading my way. Alice. *What's she doing here?* I wondered. *She's not performing today.*

"Good luck, Kirsten," she said. "I came to say good-bye."

"Good-bye?" I didn't understand.

She nodded, her eyes bright with excitement. "Vlad has arranged for me to train in Canada," she explained. "I'm leaving for Calgary in the morning."

"Wow, Alice. What does your mom say about that?"

Alice grinned. "She's staying here. I'll be living with my new coach. I'm so excited, Kirsten. Now maybe I'll be able to have fun skating again. I know it'll be tough, but at least I won't have my mom on my back all the time."

"That's great, Alice," I said. "Vlad really came through for you." I hugged her. "I wish you all the best. And don't forget to write to me. I want to hear all about your new coach and what it's like in Canada."

"Good luck to you too," she said. "Go out there and win today. You and Kai have worked so hard. No one deserves to win more than you guys. You were made for each other."

Made for each other. I liked the way that sounded.

Minutes later I met Kai and Vlad on the black padding outside the rink. Kai's eyes seemed to brighten as I came closer.

"You look beautiful, Kirsten."

"You don't look so bad yourself," I teased, taking in the dark blue turtleneck that matched my costume. The electric blue highlighted his light hair.

This time we were skating in the last group. After the scores had been tallied, Kai and I had come in sixth in the preliminary skate. We had a real chance at medaling.

"Just get out there and skate for each other," Vlad coached. "Skate as if you are the only two people in the entire universe."

Suddenly the announcer's voice boomed,

"And now, from San Mateo, California—Kirsten Hayes and Kai Bergstrom!"

"Go, Kirsten!" yelled a loud voice from the side of the rink.

I looked across and was shocked to see Troy and Tanya. They waved crazily at Kai and me, holding a bunch of roses in their hands. I beamed at them as we glided onto the ice.

The next five minutes were a total blur as we stepped out onto the huge, sparkling ice rink. The crowd grew silent as the opening chords of our music began. I counted—one, two, three, four—before I glided across the ice with Kai, flawlessly performing every jump, every spin we'd rehearsed for so long.

The music flooded over me as we prepared for our press lift. Suddenly Kai's arms supported me as I floated out above his head. The crowd was going wild. Their cheer was deafening.

My blade smoothly met the ice again as I floated down to a flawless landing. It was just like in my dreams, and I never wanted it to end.

Kai and I did a quick turn so that we were facing backward. Digging my right toe pick into the ice, I shot up into the air with incredible power. Kai and I went into our side-by-side split jumps as we spread our legs apart in a split position, reaching out to touch our toes with our fingertips. As I landed next to Kai on one foot, a huge smile crossed my face. We were one step closer to the Olympics!

We held our dramatic finishing pose in the center of the rink as flowers rained down from the bleachers and blanketed the ice. We turned toward the judges and I dropped into a graceful curtsy—Kai bowed. Then we skated off the ice as we waved to the crowd.

Kai grabbed me, spinning me around and around. He gently put me on the rubber matting and leaned down for the sweetest, most tender kiss I'd ever received.

Kai looked at me, his eyes sparkling. "We did it, Kirsten," he said. "We're a great team. On and off the ice!"

We didn't win first place that day. But it didn't matter. We came in third—and had earned a place to compete at Nationals! Kai and I had gone out for a celebratory dinner that evening with our families and Vlad. Vlad warned us that after that night, there'd be no more celebrating—we had a lot of hard work to do if we were going to do well at Nationals.

Kai and I shared a secret smile. Because we knew the same thing. Our dreams had somehow come together as one. And nothing would stop us from making our dream come true . . . just like nothing had stopped us from falling in love.

Do you ever wonder about falling in love? About members of the opposite sex? Do you need a little friendly advice but have no one to turn to? Well, that's where we come in . . . Jenny and Jake. Send us those questions you're dying to ask, and we'll give you the straight scoop on life and love in the nineties.

.

DEAR JAKE

Q: *My friend Mark is in my class and we're very close. No one knows me better than he does.*

We dated for a while, but then he told my friend that he wanted to date other people. He said I wasn't mature enough for him. That really hurt. I know I'm not the most mature girl on the planet, but I am really friendly and I love having fun. Should I try to be more mature so that he'll like me again, or should I forget about him and move on?

RT, Plymouth, Minn.

A: Talk about lack of maturity! When Mark told your friend, instead of telling you to your face, that he wanted to date other people, he took immaturity to new heights. Don't worry—you couldn't possibly surpass him in that area. Seriously, though, you shouldn't let Mark's obnoxious comments get you down. When people judge you harshly, it's usually because they feel insecure about something in themselves. Mark is probably worried about his own level of maturity. It sounds like he wasn't ready for a relationship, so he bailed out in the easiest possible way.

Above all else you should never feel you have to change for a guy. When you meet the right guy, he'll love you for who you are.

Q: *A few nights ago I went out with a guy named Quinn who I met at a teen dance. We had a blast, talking and laughing all night long. I was really nervous and he seemed to be too. Neither of us could sit still. At the end of the dance Quinn put his arm around me as he walked me to the corner for my ride. Nothing big, but it sent chills up my spine. I've had boyfriends before, but no one has ever made me feel this way.*

The problem is that he said he'd call but he hasn't. Now, every time the phone rings I go ballistic. I don't go out with my friends because I'm afraid I'll miss Quinn's call. I walk around the house, moping and daydreaming. I'm driving everyone nuts. What should I do?

BY, *Toledo, OH*

A: Rule number one in the world of dating: *Never* wait by the phone for the other person to call you. Even if you've just gone on the greatest date ever and you're about to embark on the romance of the century, it's important to have a life outside the relationship. You want to impress on the guy you're dating the fact that you're special, and that if he wants your attention he's going to have to think and plan in advance to spend time with you. So go out with your friends. If Quinn calls you and you're not there, he can leave a message.

Unfortunately, I can't predict whether or not he's going to call. It takes a certain degree of guts for a guy to take the next step in a relationship, even if the first date *was* terrific. Sometimes, when we're head over heels for someone, we chicken out. (This is a secret that most guys won't admit to, but since I'm entirely secure in my masculinity I have no problem sharing it.) Now, as to what you should do if he doesn't call back: Don't panic. If you want to, call *him*. After all, this is the nineties.

Q: *I need to know if guys go out with girls who are over-weight. I have tried everything to lose weight but nothing works. I'm tired of people talking about me behind my back. My friends tell me that if I stop eating, I'll lose weight. But I'm not sure that losing weight will be the answer. I really want a boyfriend to like me for who I am, not what I look like. Is there such a guy out there or am I fighting a losing battle?*

NN, Providence, RI

A: Do not stop eating! No one should tell you to lose weight—that decision should be yours and not your friends'. You have many qualities that make you special. So don't let other people convince you to look at yourself just in terms of your size. Everyone has strengths and weaknesses—even the people who might seem perfect on the outside.

As for the guy situation, I can assure you that guys like all kinds of girls—short, tall, heavy, skinny—even bald girls. So don't let those so-called friends of yours get you down. As long as you like who you are, there's no need to be concerned with those who want to change you. And I guarantee you'll find your Mr. Right. Until then . . . continue to work on your positive attributes and have fun hanging out with your friends.

DEAR JENNY

Q: *My friend Melissa keeps trying to set me up with guys that I don't know, and each blind date is worse than the last. The latest was Tim, a friend of Melissa's boyfriend. Tim and I went to the movies and he was all over me—holding my hand, kissing my cheek, practically saying that he was falling in love with me. Then, two days went by and he didn't call me. On the third day I called him. He said that he'd popped his shoulder out of place while lifting weights and that he couldn't dial the phone. Is that a lame excuse or what? Needless to say, he never called me back.*

Anyway, all my dates end this way. I get dumped and feel terrible. Melissa has another friend she says is perfect for me. Should I play along, say no, or just quit dating altogether?

MR, Paragould, AR

A: I can understand why you're discouraged. Tim sounds like a primo loser. If you think that's a lame excuse, what do you think of this one? "I'm sorry I never showed up for our date. I lost track of the time sorting my socks." Yes, that excuse has actually been used—on me. Or how about this one? "I got kicked in the head and forgot that I said I'd call." Part of dating is the not-so-unusual encounter with the pathological weirdo. Consider yourself lucky that Tim identified himself so soon for the flake that he is.

As for your friend Melissa, I'm afraid her taste in

guys might not be up to your standards. Unless you're getting a kick out of dipping into the pool of random (occasionally deranged) guys Melissa dredges up, this is one situation where you might be better off on your own. It's true—some of the happiest romances in history began with blind dates. But since you're obviously not having any fun, why don't you try a fresh approach?

Whatever you do, don't despair. Remember that saying about kissing a thousand frogs before meeting your prince? It's true. So get out there and do the things you like to do. Whether that's sports or photography or the school newspaper. Meeting people with similar interests is half the battle. An open attitude and a little good luck is the other half. It may take some time, but chances are you too will find a guy to be proud of—preferably one who has mastered the fine art of phone dialing.

Q: *There's this boy I like. I mean, really like. And he's a hunk. I think he wants to go out with me. But he's only in the sixth grade and I'm in the eighth.*

No one ever goes out with younger guys at my school. Am I crazy to even consider him?

GK, Santa Cruz, CA

A: At your age, a couple of years can make a huge difference. For the most part, sixth graders and eighth graders are in two completely different social worlds. The sixth graders are just starting to think about dating, while eighth graders are, well, just starting to think about dating. But eighth graders generally expect a bit more from their relationships than sixth graders.

Still, every individual is unique. I would take my time with this one. Get to know this guy better and decide for yourself whether or not he's what you're looking for in a boyfriend. So what if the other kids in your class aren't dating sixth graders. This is your life, and everyone has to follow her own dating path. But be aware that unless he's a very special guy, he may not be ready for the kind of relationship you're looking for.

Q: *Last summer I visited the Philippines. I met this cute guy named Yo. We went out just once, but it was the best date ever. Before I returned to Nevada, we promised that we'd stay in touch. When I got back to Reno, I wrote him tons of letters, but he never answered me. A month later I heard that he was going out with another girl.*

I am so hurt, but I don't want to give up on him because I think he's a very special guy. How can I keep Yo interested?

ZP, Reno, NV

A: At this point, you probably don't have a choice as far as Yo is concerned. He hasn't answered your letters and he's dating someone else, so as painful as it may be, you just have to learn to accept the fact that the fun you shared with him is over. It's natural for you to be sad right now, but you should be looking after yourself, not him.

It doesn't sound as if Yo took his promises very seriously. Since you spent so little time with him, do you think you might have mistaken Yo for who he really is? It's hard to get to know someone, and a million times harder after just one date.

At any rate, don't allow him to tie you up in your own anger. After all, Yo is just some guy who wasn't even together enough to pick up a pen and write to you about his change of heart.

Do you have questions about love? Write to:

Jenny Burgess or Jake Korman
c/o Daniel Weiss Associates
33 West 17th Street
New York, NY 10011

Watch out
Sweet Valley
University—
the Wakefield
twins are
on campus!

Jessica and Elizabeth are away
at college, with no parental
supervision! Going to classes
and parties . . . learning about
careers and college guys . . .
they're having the time of their
lives. Join your favorite twins as
they become SVU's favorite coeds!